"I promise you as long as you're with me, you're safe, Danielle."

Colt's voice was warm, the Texas drawl thick, and his gaze caught hers and held. His brown eyes softened, sweeping her face. "I just needed you to know that."

Colt Blackthorn swamped her with an emotion she couldn't process, could only drown in.

"Danielle, I need to–"

A loud crack bounced through the cab of the truck as the rear window exploded behind Colt in a hail of glass and sound.

Reaching across the cab, Colt grabbed Danielle. "Get down!"

He rammed the truck into gear and blasted across the parking lot, tires squealing, the smell of burning rubber and asphalt filling the vehicle.

The bad guys were back. For *her.*

* * *

Texas Ranger Holidays: A Season of Danger

Thanksgiving Protector by Sharon Dunn
Christmas Double Cross by Jodie Bailey
Texas Christmas Defender by Elizabeth Goddard

W9-BVN-324

Jodie Bailey writes novels about freedom and the heroes who fight for it. Her novel *Crossfire* won a 2015 RT Reviewers' Choice Best Book Award. She is convinced a camping trip to the beach with her family, a good cup of coffee and a great book can cure all ills. Jodie lives in North Carolina with her husband, her daughter and two dogs.

Books by Jodie Bailey

Love Inspired Suspense

Texas Ranger Holidays

Christmas Double Cross

Freefall
Crossfire
Smokescreen
Compromised Identity
Breach of Trust
Dead Run
Calculated Vendetta

CHRISTMAS DOUBLE CROSS

JODIE BAILEY

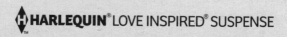

If you purchased this book without a cover you should be aware that this book is stolen property. It was reported as "unsold and destroyed" to the publisher, and neither the author nor the publisher has received any payment for this "stripped book."

Special thanks and acknowledgment to Jodie Bailey for her participation in the Texas Ranger Holidays miniseries.

Recycling programs for this product may not exist in your area.

LOVE INSPIRED BOOKS

ISBN-13: 978-0-373-45742-7

Christmas Double Cross

Copyright © 2017 by Harlequin Books S.A.

All rights reserved. Except for use in any review, the reproduction or utilization of this work in whole or in part in any form by any electronic, mechanical or other means, now known or hereinafter invented, including xerography, photocopying and recording, or in any information storage or retrieval system, is forbidden without the written permission of the editorial office, Love Inspired Books, 195 Broadway, New York, NY 10007 U.S.A.

This is a work of fiction. Names, characters, places and incidents are either the product of the author's imagination or are used fictitiously, and any resemblance to actual persons, living or dead, business establishments, events or locales is entirely coincidental.

This edition published by arrangement with Love Inspired Books.

® and TM are trademarks of Love Inspired Books, used under license. Trademarks indicated with ® are registered in the United States Patent and Trademark Office, the Canadian Intellectual Property Office and in other countries.

www.Harlequin.com

Printed in U.S.A.

Brothers and sisters, I do not consider myself yet to have taken hold of it. But one thing I do: Forgetting what is behind and straining toward what is ahead, I press on toward the goal to win the prize for which God has called me heavenward in Christ Jesus.
—Philippians 3:13-14

To Lesley...

Friend, confidante, cheerleader, truth speaker
and all-around beautiful human. You cheered
(in a parking lot!) when I finished my first book ever.
Thank you for being "my person."

I love you, girl.

ONE

Texas Ranger Colter Blackthorn shifted his borrowed Dodge Challenger into Park and left the engine running, the heater combating the near-freezing temperatures of an El Paso winter evening.

Pulling his neck to one side, he stretched the tight muscles and scanned the front of the small strip mall. The reflection of Christmas lights danced on the windows of the few cars in the lot as the center neared closing time. Somewhere in the distance a speaker piped "White Christmas" to the handful of shoppers rushing along the sidewalk on their last few days of preparation before the holiday hit full force.

He let his gaze linger on the store closest to him, on the end near the main road. Nothing moved in the shadows behind the building, but a figure moved inside by the front window, pausing to reposition a blanket beneath the *D* in Mexican Artifacts and Crafts by Danielle.

His fingers tightened on the steering wheel. It had to be her.

"Colt." The voice shot through his earpiece. Ranger Austin Brewer's voice was tight, not with anger, but with concern. "If you need to wave off, then let Major Vance know now, before you go in. We can send somebody—"

"I'm fine." His voice came out more clipped than he'd meant it to, but really, he didn't need to be babied. He was no rookie. This wasn't his first time undercover, and it wasn't as though he was going deep. All he had to do was confirm that the woman pretending to be Danielle Segovia was indeed Adriana Garcia.

The sister of notorious cartel boss Rio Garcia had been a proverbial thorn in the Rangers' sides since she'd broken ties with her brother and gone to ground. Intel said Adriana Garcia had stolen an antique watch from her brother before disappearing, one that contained a key to a storage unit housing millions in cocaine and heroin—a storage unit that was empty when the Rangers raided it. When her brother Rio discovered what she'd done, he'd gone on a rampage that had brought in the elite Texas Ranger Reconnaissance Team to bring both Garcias to justice. With their training and undercover capabilities, the team was the best option for the job.

Battling Rio had been more than enough to keep them busy since the weeks leading up to Thanksgiving. The man crossed the border at will, always managing to evade capture, and he kept a steady supply of drugs flowing, as well. Intel said he was furious with his sister and would take her back by any means necessary. When crossed, he was a vicious killer, which made finding Adriana even more important and made this mission even more dangerous.

As much as they needed to protect Adriana Garcia— and hopefully convince her to supply evidence against her brother—the Rangers also had to stop her before she started distributing the drugs from that warehouse. If she got a toehold in the drug trade in the States and started trafficking, things were going to get uglier than they already were. West Texans would not only be preyed upon by a new drug kingpin in their midst, but they'd be caught in a blood feud between a sister and brother who'd already proven themselves to be cold-blooded killers.

As far as Colt was concerned, tonight was the beginning of the Garcias' end.

"You still there?"

Colt had been quiet for too long. If he wasn't careful, Austin would have him pulled before he could do his job. "Getting into character. Adriana is smart. She's going to be looking for us."

"Well, then you'd better stop thinking of her as Adriana Garcia and start thinking of her as Danielle Segovia, or you're going to slip up."

True. Colt glanced at the phone in his hand, where a picture of a woman looked up at him, her dark hair spilling over her shoulders. Large brown eyes stared intently at the camera as she posed for a passport photo. The man in him said, under other circumstances, she'd be gorgeous.

The Ranger in him couldn't stomach the thought. All he wanted was to clasp handcuffs around her wrists and see her carted away. Forever.

Austin, of all people, should realize how important tonight was. This investigation's violence had personally touched him. Austin's fiancée, Border Patrol Agent Kylie Perry, had developed a bond with one of her informants, Valentina Hernandez, providing a college education in exchange for information. When Rio had the woman executed as a traitor, Valentina had left her baby Mercedes for Kylie to raise. No one had been ready for the chaos that ensued when the baby's father, a low-level henchman in Garcia's cartel, learned who had his daughter. Kylie, Austin, and Mercedes had all nearly paid the ultimate price.

They had survived...but Greg hadn't, thanks to Adriana. Yes, it was true that Colt's best friend Greg Gunn had turned his back on his oath as a Border Patrol officer and had aided the cartel—but that didn't mean he deserved to die.

The evidence of Greg's death in that warehouse pointed straight back to the woman who called herself Danielle Segovia, standing in a shop across the parking lot, hopefully enjoying her last few days of freedom.

"You're sure you can handle this?"

Definitely. Colt was as deeply invested in this as anyone. "Who else would we send anyway? She's seen Brent before. Alvarez is missing..." And if anything had happened to Ranger Carmen Alvarez, who'd recently vanished while undercover in the cartel, the whole team would make sure Adriana Garcia saw prison walls for the rest of her life. "The rest of the team is tied up elsewhere or lacks the experience to pull this off. It's me or nobody."

Austin huffed through the earpiece. "Listen. Greg was my friend, too. I nearly lost Kylie. You're angry. You want justice. We all do. You can't—"

"I'll call when I'm clear." Tapping the small button on the device, Colt ripped it from his ear and tossed it into the cup holder. He was tired of talking about Greg and how he'd sold himself out to the cartel. Tired of wondering when the other shoe would drop.

Tired of second-guessing his own instincts. For years, they'd gotten him where he needed to be. Until recently. He'd blown every call, starting when he missed the fact that his best friend was a traitor to his badge and his country.

That ended now. He was going to walk into that cutesy little shop where Adriana Garcia thought she was so safe, prove she was her fugitive self, and have his team on her so fast she'd never see it coming.

Then maybe he could sleep again.

With one more glance at the phone screen to cement her image in his memory, Colt tucked the device in his pocket and pushed open the door of the Challenger he'd borrowed for this operation. He missed his truck, but he couldn't drive his own vehicle for an undercover assignment, and this loaner was only for a couple of hours. Shoving his hands deep into the pockets of his black leather jacket, he kept his head down, though his eyes never stopped watching as he walked quickly across the parking lot.

Relax. He rolled his shoulders and swallowed the anger that had burned in his chest for weeks now, ever since Greg was strangled with a woman's scarf, a bracelet belonging to Adriana Garcia at his side.

Ever since Greg's fiancée revealed his treachery. The pair had worked with the Garcia cartel to fund a lavish lifestyle and bankroll their expensive wedding until Greg was murdered…and Lena tried to kill Kylie.

Wincing, Colt pulled in another stinging cold breath. Nope. Now was not the time to dwell on those memories. When he opened the door to that shop, he had to become Colter Beckett, antiques collector and big-time drug runner.

And Austin was right. For his undercover persona to be convincing, he had to think of the woman in the shop as nothing more than who she pretended to be—Danielle Segovia, small business owner.

Even if he was dead certain she was one of his team's most wanted fugitives.

A two-toned beep sounded in the back room as he pulled the door open and stepped inside, the warm air a rebellious blast against the chill outside.

No one greeted him.

Funny. Someone had been by the window a moment ago.

The shop was small, uncluttered, tastefully decorated, as though the owner took great care with each piece. Dark blue carpet, white walls and soft lighting gave the place the feel of an art gallery. Along the back wall, a low glass counter ran the width of the shop, housing small Mexican artifacts that appeared to be authentic. An open door stood behind the counter. Likely, his suspect had ducked in there.

He'd check, but he had to look like he was simply here for business. If he acted too nosy, she'd tuck tail and run, dragging the investigation back to its beginning.

Colt relaxed his shoulders, inhaling the slight smell of cinnamon and coffee that permeated the small space. Around the room, small cloth-covered tables held displays of pottery and small trinkets, most of which were replicas. Colt lifted a statuette and turned it over in his hands. Very well-done replicas. Was Adriana Garcia planning to go into counterfeiting, as well?

"May I help you?" The voice, low but confident and friendly, came from his right.

Colt reviewed a mental image of Adriana Garcia so he'd have it firmly in place when he turned toward this woman, untainted by her actual appearance. He wanted to be sure—dead sure—she was their target.

When he lifted his head, she stood near the counter. A bright red button-down shirt tucked into slim black pants accentuated her silhouette. Her height and build matched the profile. But it was the face, framed by that long dark hair, that truly caught his attention.

His heart thudded harder. He'd studied surveillance photos and official documents for days preparing for this moment.

There was no doubt. Danielle Segovia was Adriana Garcia.

She stood with one hand on the counter, her fingers curved around the back edge. Probably suspicious of everyone and wary of being caught, she likely had a gun just out of sight but at the ready.

Which meant he had to handle this delicately, when what he really wanted was to cuff her right now and drag her away. For having Kylie's informant murdered. For turning his best friend to the dark side, and then discarding him like a broken toy when he'd outlived his usefulness. For a thousand other crimes they could pin squarely on the woman who stood in front of him with an air of fake innocence and manufactured friendliness.

But he couldn't. Forcing a smile, he settled the statuette gently back to its pedestal and stepped toward her, keeping his posture relaxed even though every muscle in his body wanted to fight. At his side, the heft of his pistol tugged, a comfort as he stood facing a woman who'd dealt death without mercy.

Her past exploits said it all.

If Colt made one wrong move, there would be a gun battle. And in all likelihood, neither of them would survive.

Danielle Segovia tightened her fingers around the edge of the counter until the glass dug into her palm and tried to tell herself there was nothing to worry about. Likely, the man who was setting off every one of her internal alarm bells was browsing her shop right before closing only a few days before Christmas looking for a last-minute gift for his wife.

Except he wasn't wearing a wedding ring.

His girlfriend then. Her shop wasn't cheap, which surely meant he was buying a present for someone he liked enough to splurge on. So why did she sense so much anger behind his eyes?

She kept her eyes from drifting to the can of Mace she'd purchased to appease her younger brother Justin, who kept insisting she buy a pistol instead. Since the shop had been ransacked by vandals a couple of weeks before, she'd felt eyes on her all of the time. Probably paranoia. Most likely nothing.

But this guy... He radiated a tension she couldn't ignore.

The man looked at her without raising his head, his brown eyes finding hers under lashes that it was so not fair a man had gotten. His hair was short, but not military short like some of the soldiers from Fort Bliss. He was built like one of them, though. Even though he wore a dark leather jacket, she could tell. He was strong.

Muscular. Like he'd earned his physique and not just sweated it out in a gym.

A slight smile tilted the corner of his mouth—knowing, almost like he'd read her thoughts from across the room.

Her face had better not be pinking up the way it felt. Danielle cleared her throat. "Were you looking for something in particular?"

"I'm sorry." He finally lifted his chin, and the smile he'd quirked tilted both sides of his mouth. "I was noticing the replica you have here. It's a very good one."

"Thank you. I've been working in pottery and sculpture for years." Finally, her stomach unclenched. If he was dangerous, he'd have attacked by now. "If you're interested, that one's not for sale, but I have some similar ones I can show you."

He lifted the statuette again and cradled it gently, almost as though he understood the value it possessed. "What's so special about this one?"

His gentleness undid the last of her apprehension, and she crossed the room toward him, standing on the other side of the pedestal where the piece usually rested, close enough to smell the spice of his cologne. "It has my mother's thumbprint on the bottom." She held out her hand and he laid the piece in it so she could turn it over and point to the small print at the corner of the base. "It's the last one we did together before she died."

"I'm sorry to hear that." The stranger nodded and took the statue back, running his thumb along the print, his eyes following the motion. "I understand, though. I lost someone close to me when I was a teenager. And if I had something like this…" He stopped, cleared his throat and settled the piece back onto the pedestal before he looked at her again, a teasing glint replacing the somber expression he'd worn a moment earlier. "So, would you happen to have one with *your* thumbprint on it?"

Wow. Just when she'd thought he might be different than all the rest, he had to go and flirt with her. Awkwardly. "Sorry. No." Danielle huffed out a breath, done with this conversation. "I'm about to close. Were you interested in something or were you just ducking in to get out of the cold?"

"Actually, I *was* looking for something." Seeming to realize he'd gone too far, he took a step away from her and surveyed the room as though he knew exactly what he wanted. "A buddy of mine was in here a couple of weeks ago and said you had a standing stone figure from Mezcala."

It was the most expensive piece she possessed, on consignment from an elderly woman at her church. The hairs on the back of her neck stood up. What did this man want, showing up late, asking specifically about the stone figure so soon after someone ransacked the place looking for…something? "I have one on consignment, but it's not here. It's a rare piece, and the shop is not secure enough to house it. If you'd like to see it, I can make arrangements for us to meet elsewhere, but I should tell you the owner is asking for ten thousand, and she's not willing to negotiate that price." Actually, if left on her own with a smooth talker, Senora Noguerra would likely wind up giving the priceless artifact away. That was the main reason Danielle had convinced the older lady to let her handle the sale, even though she didn't generally work with consignments or deal in artifacts worth that much money.

"Understandable. If you have a business card, I can call you after the holidays and set up a time. I definitely want to see it. If someone else expresses interest before we can meet, let them know I'll beat any price."

"Certainly." Her voice stayed level. Amazing, given the way her chest tightened in anticipation. She'd get Senora Noguerra a good price, maybe even higher than she'd dreamed, and finally allow the elderly lady some breathing room in her finances. Danielle pulled a card from her pocket and handed it over.

He took it by the edge and glanced at it. "Danielle Segovia." When he lifted his eyes again, he found hers immediately, reading her expression. The full force of those brown eyes was almost more than she could handle. She nodded and said a quick prayer he'd leave soon, before she asked him to walk next door for coffee or something stupid like that.

Which she couldn't do. Justin was due back to the apartment soon, and Danielle had a few things to say about the late nights her younger brother had been keeping lately. She'd gotten the automatic email from the school today. His grades were dipping. This wasn't the time to be flirting with a man, even if he did take the time to honor her mother's memory, unlike everyone else who came in and plunked the statue down when they found out it wasn't genuine.

The stranger extended his hand. "I'm Colter Beckett." His grip was strong and warm, and he held on tightly for an instant longer than he should have, spiking electricity up her arm before he pulled away. "I'll talk to you in a few days." He turned and left the store, disappearing up the sidewalk toward the end of the building.

Danielle slumped against the pedestal and whistled low. Wow. Wait until she told Zoe about this guy. She balled her fist to hold on to the warmth of his hand, then shook it out just as quickly. Stupid. She had better things to do than give in to the impulse to run to the window and watch Colter Beckett walk away.

She had a fifteen-year-old brother to raise.

Puffing out one more breath, Danielle locked the front of the shop and killed the lights. Grabbing her purse from the back, she set the alarm and stepped out into the chilled El Paso night, straining to see the stars overhead. If this cold snap kept up much longer, they might actually get snow for Christmas. A genuine rarity.

As she pulled her keys from her purse, an engine started in the small alley behind the shop. When she lifted her head, headlights blinded her.

Danielle froze instinctively, even as she tried to tell herself that there was no reason to believe she was in danger. Maybe it was some kids using her back lot to hang out. Maybe one of the cops who'd said they'd drive by after the break-in had finally made good on the promise. It would be the first time.

But then a huge man, broad and bulky, stepped into the headlights and stalked toward her, his silhouette a hulk in the brightness.

Danielle backed up two steps before she bumped into the locked door of her shop, dropping her purse. She turned to run for the parking lot.

But the man was faster. A thick arm wrapped around her waist and jerked her backward against a beefy chest, crushing the air from her lungs before she could scream.

TWO

"It's her." Colt switched the phone to his earpiece then turned the key in the ignition, speaking before Austin could say hello. "I had her give me a business card. We can pull a print to be sure. I'm to get in touch with her after the holiday, and we'll see how much intel I can gather before we take her in. Once she trusts me as a runner for hire, we're in."

"Brent's not going to like this."

The muscle under Colt's eye jumped, the place where his stress seemed to show the most. Ranger Brent McCord had once been a close friend, but this Adriana Garcia thing had fractured that friendship. McCord said the woman had once saved his life, and based on that single encounter, he refused to credit any of the evidence against her—even when it came to Greg's murder.

Colt didn't dispute that her actions had prevented Brent's execution…but she'd probably had some darker, hidden motive for it. A woman who could kill so indiscriminately would only save a Ranger if the choice in some way benefitted her. Maybe she'd even planned for this to happen—for Brent's defense of her to create cracks in their Ranger team.

"He saw Adriana Garcia five years ago for under two minutes. Not enough time to be a reliable judge of her character. Brent needs to remember to be objective."

"So do you."

"This woman is the reason Valentina Hernandez was killed. She killed Greg with—"

"Nobody knows the stakes more than I do, Blackthorn. Believe me." Austin ground out the words. "But we don't have concrete proof that Adriana killed Greg. No matter what we feel, we have to remember, innocent until—"

"Got it."

"Loosen up, or you're going to tip her off. Either that, or Vance is going to pull all of us and bring in another team."

"I said I've got it." Only Colt wasn't so certain anymore. Through his whole career, his instincts had been his guide. He was known as the man who could feel danger before it happened. Now? He'd missed the fact that his best friend was a traitor. Colt dropped his head against the headrest and glared at the ceiling.

But he was right this time. As pleasant as she seemed, as soft as her eyes had gotten when she'd spun that story about her mother, as much as her supposed grief had tugged for just a second at Colt's own, he knew they had their woman.

With a deep breath, he reached for his seat belt and tilted his head forward, movement catching at the edges of his vision.

At the back of the shopping center, a man dragged a woman toward a dark blue two-door sedan that had seen better days.

The woman twisted and fought with all she had.

With a massive head thrust backward, she caught the brute in the jaw and broke free, crashing to her knees on the cracked asphalt, a dark curtain of hair falling across her face.

Recognition jolted through Colt and his jaw tightened as he ran through his options for intervening. Jump out and run for the fight without knowing what he was getting into, or gun the engine and blow in through tire-squealing smoke.

The would-be captor reached down and hauled Colt's suspect to her feet, backhanding her so hard she fell against the open trunk of the car, where he stuffed her in the rest of the way and slammed the lid.

No time to make it on foot now.

"We've got trouble." He clicked his seat belt and jammed the car into Drive, tires squealing as he gunned the engine and raced toward the man trying to take their suspect away. The blood rushed hot in his veins as he relayed what he was seeing to Austin, who called for backup.

He couldn't let the driver get away. The team was counting on him to bring Adriana in. Professionally, they needed to know where she was stashing the drugs she'd stolen from her brother so they could keep the supply from hitting the market. Personally, he knew that only her confession could truly give him closure about Greg's death.

At the sound of the roaring engine, the passenger leapt into the blue car as the driver whirled toward Colt and lifted his arm.

Colt instinctively ducked as a bullet ricocheted off the roof. The others went wide. He didn't slow, aiming head-on in a game of chicken, man versus machine.

Colt knew he had more nerve than the brute stealing one of Rangers' most wanted had ever dreamed.

Sure enough, the other man dove into his front seat and gunned the engine, whipping the car into a skid and racing down the narrow alley behind the shops toward the back service road.

This had to stop before they went too far and hit the main road, where bystanders could get hurt.

"Status?" Austin had clearly heard the hit.

"I'm right behind him." Colt called out street names as the lead car hung a right, deeper into an older neighborhood. The highway waited on the other side.

As Colt skidded the Challenger around the corner and gunned the engine to keep up with the small sedan, the passenger leaned out the window, firing wildly at Colt.

"Are you kidding me?" He muttered under his breath. This guy was an idiot.

"What?"

"We're in a very bad action movie here. Get me some backup before this guy kills somebody. We're way too close to Gateway Boulevard."

"Local law enforcement is on the way. Hang on."

A wild shot pinged off the passenger mirror, and Colt pulled into the other lane, one eye on the lookout for oncoming traffic on the narrow neighborhood street and one on the kidnappers. His engine had a whole lot more power than the ancient beat up two-door he was tailing. If he could get closer, maybe he'd be able to tap the rear corner and spin the vehicle.

But if the car flipped, or spun and hit anything trunk first, then the woman masquerading as Danielle Segovia could be killed.

More blood on his hands.

Colt gripped the steering wheel tighter, maintaining enough distance to keep the passenger from getting a clear shot but close enough to hold his options open. If they got to Gateway where a higher volume of traffic became a factor, he could lose them. Worse, someone else could be killed.

This had to be Rio Garcia's men, out to bring his sister in for stealing from the cartel. If they somehow managed to cross the border or they reached the airport... "Tell the LEOs to get in tight at the airport. And let Border Patrol know not to let this guy cross. If he somehow manages to get away from me——"

"They might kill her."

"No. They want her alive. They won't find out where Garcia's money or drugs are if she's dead."

"On it."

Think, Blackthorn. He had to stop this guy. For the past week, he'd cruised these streets, looking for potential ways Danielle Segovia could escape, planning for a moment when he'd have to give chase if she ran. Now he'd have to show his hand and use his knowledge not to capture her, but to save her.

Another bullet pinged off the passenger door. It was now or never. Punching the pedal to the floor, Colt raced up on the rear of the sedan and roared past to the next intersection, pulling the car into a skid that left him facing the other car, leaving the driver with nowhere to go except through Colt.

Another game of chicken. His heart pounded as the headlights roared closer. He held the steering wheel tight. If he died trying to save a killer...

The blue sedan skidded to the side, the driver's door

slamming into the corner of a Dumpster, sliding the massive hulk of metal backward as the car bounced to an abrupt stop.

Dust peppered the air as Colt threw open the door of the sports car and ran for the other vehicle. One look at the driver was more than enough to haunt his nightmares for a very long time. Without air bags or a seatbelt, he'd felt the full force of the Dumpster's crushing blow.

The wavering smell of gasoline permeated the air. He was running out of time.

The passenger door hung open, the seat empty, and pounding feet raced between the two buildings closest to Colt. A trail of blood droplets led from the scene. The passenger might be hurt, but he was fast and chasing after him would take time Colt didn't have to spare. As much as Colt would love to pursue, there were bigger things to worry about. With gas leaking from the vehicle, anything could happen before he got the woman out of the trunk.

As sirens wailed in the distance, closing fast, he reached across and pulled the keys from the ignition, then rounded the rear of the vehicle. Popping the key in the lock, he held his breath, praying that what he found inside wouldn't be as bad as he feared.

The woman lay in the corner, her arms wrapped around her knees. She shook uncontrollably, eyes wide with fear as she stared up at Colt. "Please…" The word rasped from a dry throat and tugged at Colt's conscience.

Gently, Colt scooped her into his arms as several black and white El Paso police Chargers raced toward the scene, their red and blue lights flashing in the night.

She clung to him, her fingers digging into his arms as she shuddered repeatedly. She was in shock. Terrified.

The ambulance hadn't arrived yet, and Colt had to get her to the hospital. Sliding her gently into the front seat of his car, he buckled her in and shut the door, then turned to answer to the police officers who skidded to a stop in front of him. Although identifying himself as a Ranger could jeopardize his entire undercover persona, he had no choice. He had to make sure Adriana survived.

Slamming the door of the sports car, Colt stared over the top at the entrance to the emergency room where, not three minutes earlier, nurses and orderlies had rushed his suspect into the hospital.

His goal had been to keep her close during transport and to stay by her side at the hospital, but he'd lost her anyway when medical personnel refused to let him follow her. Right now, she could be making her way out some entrance he couldn't see.

Colt slammed his palm onto the car's roof. Nothing was going the way he'd thought it would. He should have known something was wrong before she was attacked, should have been able to sense it in the air. But no. He'd missed this attempt on their suspect's life, just like he'd missed Greg's treachery.

Tipping his head toward the sky, where the stars were muted by the lights of downtown El Paso, he shook his head. Greg. They'd been best friends for years. Fate, God, whatever you wanted to call it, had led them to work together on a few cases, had made them buddies. Cookouts. Football games. All of that male bonding stuff. Colt was supposed to be the best man at his wedding, which had been planned for only a few short days from today.

Now, as the wedding date drew near, Greg's fiancée was behind bars for attempting to kill Kylie Perry.

And Greg was dead. A traitor to his country, a man who'd taken a small fortune in order to turn his head as drug runners crossed the very borders he'd sworn to defend.

Dead. At the hands of the woman who was somewhere in the guts of the hospital in front of him.

Dragging his hand from the top of the car, Colt's finger caught in the divot left behind when a bullet had bounced off the roof. He winced and stepped back, for the first time inspecting the black Challenger. The roof had taken a couple of hits. The metal along the passenger side of the windshield sported damage, and a crack wound its way across the top of the windshield on the driver's side.

He whistled low between pursed lips. Thought about thanking God for not letting any of those hit him. Decided against it. It wasn't like God was paying attention anyway.

But Major Vance sure would be, and he wasn't going to like it when Colt brought back yet another loaner with damage.

It wasn't like he could help it. Getting involved in a shootout hadn't been part of the plan.

Neither was losing their target.

He jogged across the parking lot, determined to find Adriana even if it meant going toe to toe with anyone who tried to stand in his way. He'd likely tipped his hand by showing off his skills in the chase and his badge to the police when he'd rescued her. He sure didn't need her running now.

Just before the entrance, a shrill whistle echoed off the buildings. His feet slowed and his jaw set. He knew that sound. Knew who was behind it.

He wasn't ready for this fight. Not now.

Before Colt stopped, he caught his breath and swallowed his frustration. No need to take this annoyance out on his teammates, even if they didn't see eye to eye on this one.

When he turned, Brent McCord was almost at his side, his expression dark, his brown hair wild under his Stetson as though he'd ridden all the way here with the windows down.

Behind Brent, Ford Manning kept his gaze on the parking lot, his cowboy hat shading his face so that Colt couldn't read his expression. He probably didn't want to play peacemaker between his two teammates.

Colt jerked his head toward the door. "She's inside. I'm on my way to find out where."

"How is she?" Brent's words were rushed, urgent. "She hurt?"

Balling his fists, Colt fought the urge to bite out a sarcastic response. "I don't know. She was in shock when I pulled her out of the trunk, but she was conscious, coherent. The guy who stuffed her in the trunk hit her pretty hard though, and that was before that wild ride she took."

"Was wrecking the car with her in the trunk your only option?"

That was it. Colt stepped closer to Brent, meeting green eyes at the exact same height as his own. "Would you prefer I opened fire? Took the risk of shooting her?"

His voice was low, the words gravel in his mouth. Challenging Brent was another blow to his emotions, but he wasn't going to be questioned. Not now. Not when the stakes were this high. "You weren't there. I did the best I could. I'm sorry you're girlfr—"

"Okay, enough." Ford appeared in Colt's peripheral vision and laid a hand on each man's shoulder. "Do I need to remind you again that you're on the same side? Or that you're in public in front of the hospital and two of us are dressed in uniform so the whole world can identify us on social media as brawling Rangers?"

Colt hesitated half a second, then took a step back, hating that Ford was right on both counts. Bad publicity for the department was the last thing they needed. "Fine."

Brent didn't back down, but he did ease his stance, looking a little less like he was about to put a fist into Colt's jaw. "Look, we have a problem."

"From where I stand, we have a lot of problems." Number one being their most wanted suspect was out of sight while they stood here debating her guilt.

"Enough." Ford repeated the word, then shook his head. "I'm not the daddy of either one of you, but I'll knock some sense into both of you if I have to."

That did it. Colt's mouth tipped into a grin, but it faded just as quickly. "What's the problem?"

"Major Vance had a few of our guys track Danielle Segovia to a routine physical and was able to get a blood sample from the doctor a few days ago. We rushed it through and Lizzie just called. The DNA doesn't match what we found at Greg's crime scene."

Colt took two more steps back, his hands loose at his sides. He wasn't hearing this. If the DNA didn't match, that meant Danielle Segovia wasn't at the scene where Greg Gunn was killed. Or at least, that wasn't her DNA on the scarf used to strangle him. "That doesn't mean she didn't kill Greg, and it doesn't mean she's not Adriana Garcia. With the Garcia name behind her, she can get plenty of henchmen to do her dirty work. We have that bracelet, too, the one she was wearing in surveillance videos and found right next to Greg's body. Right there, we've got proof—"

"Convenient proof—maybe even planted." Brent paced up the sidewalk away from the door and motioned for the other two men to follow.

Not this again. Colt glanced at the glass door, itching to head inside and find out where the supposed Danielle Segovia was before she vanished like smoke.

Ford jerked his head toward Brent and waited for Colt to follow.

He bristled at being treated like a bratty teenager, then puffed out a breath. He deserved it. He was acting like one.

Brent turned and pinned Colt with a hard gaze. "I still say her brother set her up. Rio Garcia wants his sister alive. She has his stash and he needs it back. If he set up Adriana, then all he has to do is watch where we go and we'll lead him right to her."

"He'll have to be watching close." Colt didn't buy the whole *Adriana Garcia is innocent* thing. Brent was infatuated with a killer. "It would be hard for him to track us."

"There's no reason to think he doesn't have somebody else on the inside. He had Greg."

"Hey, now. Low blow there, McCord." Ford's drawl cut into the conversation before Colt could bristle and respond. Ford turned to Colt. "Ethan's on his way over. He swept the area behind the store, and we're waiting for a team to go into the Segovia apartment. He found her purse—she dropped it in the struggle. But he said the only ID in this girl's wallet is Danielle Segovia. No links to Adriana Garcia at all."

Colt wasn't ready to believe the woman he'd hauled to the hospital babbling about her brother wasn't their suspect. "We've been through this already. You and I both know how easy it is to manufacture a fake identity." He was done here. He had an assignment and, right now, it lay inside that hospital, not out here rehashing what they already knew. "Y'all do what you have to do out here. I'm going to make sure Danielle Segovia or Adriana Garcia or whatever her name is doesn't slip out while we're not looking."

Before either of his teammates could argue, he stalked toward the door, falling in behind a young kid with floppy dark hair, wearing a black T-shirt and blue jeans, who rushed to the counter ahead of Colt.

The kid reached for ID and passed it to the security guard at the desk. "I'm looking for my sister, Danielle Segovia."

Colt froze. Adriana Garcia only had one brother. Rio. This kid was definitely not the cartel lord. He edged closer and glanced at the ID on the counter. Justin Segovia. The same address as Danielle's apartment.

If Danielle Segovia really was Adriana Garcia, then who was this kid? And what did he want with her?

THREE

Danielle's head pounded.

No. That wasn't it.

She squeezed her eyes shut tighter. It wasn't just her head. It was every part of her body. Even her hair hurt. For sure her head took the prize, though. Every time she managed to crack her eyes open, the light in the hospital room drilled into her skull. But mixed in with the pain was fear.

What had happened to the man who had manhandled her to the ground? Was he still here? Waiting for her? Lurking in the hallway? Her memories were too muddled to make any sense. She remembered darkness. Chaotic, whirling darkness. Slamming against objects. A dull roar that rose and fell until it lapsed into eerie, shuddering silence with a final crash. Then…light. And a face she recognized, arms lifting and cradling her as she tried to bring reality back into focus.

The man from her shop. He'd spoken very little, only a few words she couldn't piece together. He'd brought her to the hospital.

He'd saved her life.

Why?

Her breaths came faster. Maybe he was in on the attack against her.

But no. His face when he'd spoken of her mother… No. He wasn't that kind of man. Haunted maybe, but not evil.

Not like the man who'd apparently tried to kill her.

She fought to sit up, wanting to feel less vulnerable and helpless, but her muscles protested. Her whole body was too heavy to move, the pain amplifying her panic.

Gentle hands on her shoulders eased her back, and someone laid a hand on the top of her head. "Dani. It's okay. You're safe."

Dani. Only one person was allowed to call her that.

Relaxing into the pillows, she turned her face toward the voice. "Lights?"

"Want me to see if I can turn 'em off?"

She nodded slightly and the sound of his feet in those ever-present Vans padded across the room, then the light in front of her eyelids dimmed considerably. She eased them open as her brother sat in a chair beside the bed and slouched against the back, stretching his legs out.

Danielle almost smiled, and would have if her jaw didn't ache so badly. Now that he knew she was awake, all signs of concern or affection from Justin would probably cease. They were in public, after all.

The twinge of amusement didn't last long. His brown eyes were dark with something that had to be fear as he stared at her. His too-long brown hair fell over the creases in his forehead. He was upset, even if he'd never say it out loud.

"I'm fine. Really. Don't look at me like that." Even though it was painful, Danielle pressed the button to ease the bed up, trying to prove to both of them that she'd survived the ordeal mostly unscathed. Still, if she hurt this bad tonight, what would tomorrow feel like?

"Somebody tried to kidnap you. They stuffed you in a trunk, Dani. And when that car wrecked, you could have been…" He shoved out of the chair and paced to the window, shoving his hand through the mop of hair she kept begging him to cut. "Somebody has to look out for you. I should have been at the shop tonight."

Fear threatened to rip Danielle's chest open, but she managed to keep her voice level. In spite of her own trauma, she had to stay strong for her brother. He'd been through enough, losing both parents when he was younger. Nearly losing his sister in a car accident had to be weighing on him now. But she was entitled to her fear, too, and the thought of those dangerous men anywhere near her brother twisted her stomach into knots. "What were you going to do? You're fifteen, and those guys had guns."

"Maybe I should start carrying."

"Absolutely not."

"All I'm saying is—"

"No." She pushed every ounce of the parental authority the state had given her into her voice. "All *I'm* saying is you're too young. And you're letting that crew you hang around with fill your head with the idea—"

"They'd have helped me save you tonight."

"They'll drag you to jail with them." She'd seen him on the corner and in the little Mexican take-out place in the shopping center, hanging out with a whole new group of friends who gave her insomnia. They were a rough bunch. While she believed Justin hadn't done anything crazy yet, sometimes she thought it was only a matter of time before they convinced her soft-hearted brother that he needed the group's "protection." Or their cash. They flashed a lot of it. Was that what drew him? "Justin—"

"The cops want to ask you some questions. Wanted to know when you had your head on straight and were awake." He huffed out a sigh without turning away from the window. "I'll go tell them you're back to your old self again."

She huffed. The police hadn't been any help so far. "I won't talk to them."

"Dani, you have to. They'll find these guys so they don't hurt you again. Somebody has to figure out why this happened."

"*Somebody* has been zero help since the shop was hit by vandals. For whatever reason, the police aren't doing anything. When they do talk to me, they treat me like I did something wrong. Tell them to go away."

"I won't." He whipped around so fast his hair flopped across his forehead. "Somebody tried to kidnap you. Don't you think that's a little bit worse than tearing apart the store? You know what they keep talking about at school, warning the girls about? It's not drugs these guys are after now. It's pretty girls. Young girls. Wanna know why?"

"Stop it." Nausea whirled in her stomach, overwhelming the pain with a fear that might take her out. If those guys were human traffickers…

Justin's expression softened and he came back to her, resting his hand on her head again, the way their father had done when they were kids. "Help stop these guys. Make sure they don't target somebody else, somebody who doesn't have a hero willing to chase them down. One of them… One of them got away."

"Then they can question the other one."

His fingers tightened on her scalp. "The driver's dead. He didn't have an ID on him."

Dead. It was a final, awful word, even for a man who had harmed her. "Who told you that?"

"The guy who saved your life." His words bit off at the end. He was trying to bury his fear underneath anger.

Danielle's eyes widened. "He's here?"

"At the end of the hall in a huddle with a bunch of official-looking types. I think he's a cop. Or something bigger. There's some cowboy hats, boots, leather belts out there…"

Texas Rangers? They handled things the police wouldn't touch.

Maybe that was what she needed. "I'll talk to Colter Beckett. But only him. Nobody else comes in this room." Something in his demeanor at the store had tugged at her, had said that despite the odd air about him, she could trust him.

And he had, after all, been the one to rescue her.

Justin headed for the door, then stopped at the entrance and hung his head. He glanced back at her, all traces of his earlier anger and frustration gone. "I'm glad you're okay. If you weren't…"

If she could get out of bed and go to him, she would. Even if he tried to pull away, she'd hug him hard enough to reassure both of them. "God's got us, Justin."

"Sure He does." He was gone before she could say anything else.

Spent after trying to be strong for him, Danielle shut her eyes and let the weight of her head pull her into the pillow. All she wanted was to go home, but she hadn't seen a doctor or a nurse to ask how long she'd be here.

A soft tap at the door opened her eyes again.

Colter Beckett stood there. Tall. Muscular. His brown eyes just as unreadable now as they had been in the shop. But the set of his jaw was a whole lot different.

Guarded. Cautious. Angry.

But at whom?

Stepping into the room, he shut the door and strode in with a defiant confidence he hadn't carried earlier. He stopped at the foot of her bed and looked down at her as though he was holding back a whole lot of what he really wanted to say.

She suddenly wished she hadn't let him in the room.

With practiced efficiency, he held out identification that included the familiar star-shaped badge of the Texas Rangers. "Ranger Colter Blackthorn. Who were those men?"

The abrupt question tensed her shoulders and raked across her already aching head. "I'm sorry?"

"Did you recognize either one of them? Have you seen them before? Anywhere?"

Danielle shook her head, her eyebrows furrowing and tugging on the bruise that was bound to be forming in her check and jaw. Something was wrong. The way he was looking at her, questioning her... It was exactly like the police had treated her when the shop was vandalized.

She wasn't the victim in his mind.

Somehow, she was the criminal.

The barely controlled anger coursing through Colt wasn't something he was used to. Looking down at the woman who was responsible for so much betrayal and death and pain... His fingers wrapped around the hard plastic at the foot of the bed and dug in, his jaw clenched so tight the tension radiated into his temples.

She had no right to look up at him with eyes so wide and frightened, tugging at his sympathy and making him want to ease up on his questions. He was starting to understand how Brent could have fallen for her manipulations. But he wouldn't be that easily trapped.

He pulled a deep breath in through his nose and fixed his gaze on hers.

She shrunk further into herself. For half a second, he almost relented, but then he remembered who he was dealing with. A woman cold-blooded enough to kill for what she wanted, greedy enough to funnel drugs into the country without care for the harm she was doing.

Colt forced his jaw to work. "If I were you, I'd start talking now, *Danielle*." Her name ground out on a wave of sarcasm so heavy, it nearly sank in the air. "We already have the warrant for your apartment. Your prints and DNA are being run as we speak, courtesy of that same warrant. You're caught. It's over."

Her mouth opened, closed. Wide brown eyes narrowed, a deep V writing confusion between her eyes as she shook her head. "What is... I don't..." She exhaled loudly and leaned her head back toward the ceiling, muttering something softly in Spanish. Colt picked up only a few words. *Jesus. Help me.*

Wow. She was a better actress than he'd thought. She'd have to be to fool Rio, who wasn't known for being the trusting type. But appealing to Jesus? Colt hadn't been on speaking terms with God in many years, but even he knew that was a low blow.

Still, she looked helpless. Scared.

The fear in her eyes drew him, made him want to dial back his aggression and comfort her, make her feel better.

But she couldn't drag him in. He'd long ago grown cold.

Tucking his elbows closer to his sides, he pulled his gaze from her to a spot just above her head. Forgetting who he was dealing with would be dangerous. "Why me? Why talk to me?"

"Because I thought you were someone who could be trusted. When it comes to the authorities, I'm picky lately."

She'd found her voice, and it was rising fast.

"Seems to me, if I were you, I'd be picky, too." Colt let himself pin her eyes again. "You chose the wrong person to trust, because I'm the one you ought to fear the most."

Her eyes widened as her head jerked back. She winced from the movement, tears edging to the corners of her eyes.

He turned his head to look out the window at the El Paso skyline. "Listen, I'll lay it out for you. What we want is—"

"Colt." The voice came from behind him, low and loaded with authority.

Forcing his fingers to unlock from the foot of the bed, Colt turned to face Austin Brewer, who stood in the doorway, imposing in his unofficial uniform of khaki pants and a white button-down, his Stetson at his side. Normally, Austin was smiling, but not now. Something in his expression said things had gotten a whole lot worse than someone trying to kidnap the suspect the Rangers had been hunting.

His gut twisted. Was it Carmen? Since going undercover in the Garcia cartel over a month ago, Ranger Carmen Alvarez had been missing. No contact. No nothing. The greatest fear among the team was that she'd been taken… Or worse. And the look on Austin's face right now hinted that Colt might need to steel himself.

If they'd lost Carmen because of the woman behind him… He fisted his hands and walked toward Austin, who fell into step beside him.

"You can't question her like that. You're way out of line." Austin kept his voice low, a reminder, not a reprimand.

Digging his teeth into his lower lip, Colt stayed quiet. Austin spoke the truth. They had to tread lightly or a technicality would wreck this case in court.

"Now come with me—there are some things you should know," Austin continued, leading Colt a short distance up the hallway where Rangers Trevor Street and Ethan Hilliard waited.

Trevor's glance raked over Colt's then stuck to a bulletin board on the wall, something like pity, maybe even frustration, in the look.

Ethan just watched.

"Carmen?" Colt wasn't going to wait for someone to lob the grenade. He was going to pull the pin himself.

Ethan shook his head. "No word on that front."

That was either good…or very, very bad. Bad news meant closure. No news meant she was still out there, and no one knew her condition. But Colt knew Carmen. She was smart. Tough. Savvy enough to keep from being found out. Knowing her, she was hiding, waiting for the right time to come in and blow this whole thing wide open.

If that was the case, why did everyone look as though someone had keyed their pickups?

Austin blew out a loud breath and scratched the top of his head. "No easy way to say this, Blackthorn."

"Then spit it out."

"That woman is not Adriana Garcia. Not even close."

Colt backed off and stalked up the hallway away from his teammates, dragging his hand through his hair. No way. The woman in that hospital bed had to be Adriana Garcia. The photo wouldn't lie. Neither would his gut.

Except his gut had proven wrong one too many times recently, which was probably why Trevor couldn't look him in the eye.

Colt turned back to his team but didn't step closer. "Prove it."

"The print we lifted off the business card? It belongs to Danielle Segovia. The same one that's been showing up in the database all along. Twenty-six. Born and raised here in El Paso. Mother was Mexican. Father an American she met when he was stationed at Bliss. Both died in a car wreck a few years ago. She's raising a younger brother. We have school records, taxes filed. She's solid. The print doesn't match Garcia's."

"A good cover." Except fingerprints didn't typically lie.

"There's more. Lizzie called. Preliminary DNA testing on the blood found in the car's trunk is way off. Danielle Segovia is not even a twelfth cousin to the Garcias."

The words hit Colt in the chest, forcing the air from

his lungs. He gripped his cheeks and dragged his hand along his mouth, tugging at the tension in his jaws. "So why did someone try to take her?"

"Same reason we came after her. Same reason local law enforcement tipped us when she called them about the break-in at her store and she looked just like the BOLO we put out on Adriana." Ethan straightened and shoved his hands in his pockets. "I glanced through the window of the room just now while you two were talking." He held his phone up, open to the passport photo of Adriana Garcia that they all carried. "She's a dead ringer, right down to the way she parts her hair."

Trevor sniffed and finally spoke. "Which means Manning and Rook are at the wrong apartment right now, searching for evidence they're never going to find."

"Major Vance already called them off," Ethan said. "They're headed here, because we've got bigger problems in that hospital room right now."

Colt dropped his chin and shook his head. *Bigger problems* was an understatement. Not only had they not found the woman half of the state was hunting, they'd led Rio Garcia here and put a civilian in danger. That meant Danielle Segovia was one more complication in the hunt for Adriana Garcia.

One that could prove deadly for the woman they had placed in harm's way.

FOUR

Pain, fear and confusion spun into a cocktail that threatened to swamp Danielle.

When the door closed behind the two men, the tension in the room dropped palpably. Danielle sank into the pillow and closed her eyes, willing the world to stop spinning. A Texas Ranger had gone undercover in her shop, then rescued her from kidnappers only to interrogate her now. This had to be a trauma-induced nightmare. The way he'd talked to her, it was clear that he believed she'd done something wrong, but he'd never said what it was.

The only thing she knew with certainty was that she wanted out of here before Colter Blackthorn came back. If he started in on her again, she didn't know what she'd do. Too much had happened in the past few hours. The last thing she needed was to fall apart in front of the angry Ranger. He'd probably view the weakness as some sort of confession.

Her finger hovered over the call button for the nurse. They couldn't keep her here. She could refuse treatment, tell them she wanted to be discharged. There were plenty of people from church who'd be willing to drive her home.

But the Rangers knew where to find her. This wouldn't be over until they got whatever it was they wanted from her.

Dropping her hand to the bed beside her, Danielle gave up and closed her eyes. She'd have to ride this out and pray she didn't wind up in jail for someone else's crimes.

Jesus, I don't know what's going on. I don't understand anything that's happened tonight. But, Lord, give Colter Blackthorn the truth about me. Don't let me go to jail and leave Justin on his own.

There it was. Her biggest fear. If something happened to her, who would take care of her brother? Especially now, when he was spending more and more time with those friends of his who now had him believing he needed a gun at fifteen. None of this boded well.

Two light taps on the door drifted across the room, followed by a slight shuffling sound.

Danielle didn't even open her eyes. It was probably the doctor. Finally. He could discharge her and get her out of here.

"Ms. Scgovia?" The male voice was quiet, but its speaker was unmistakable.

Danielle stiffened. He was back.

She had a choice. Knuckle under and collapse in front of him or put up the brave front she'd used when her parents died, the one that had gotten her custody of her brother when she'd fought for him in front of the family court judge.

Easing her eyes open, Danielle prepared for battle. She wasn't backing down to a lie. Fixing a hard gaze on

Colt, she bit out her next words. "I have nothing more to say to you." The fire was unfamiliar on her tongue. She was used to being customer-service-oriented and friendly at all times, used to cooperating with law enforcement even when they didn't cooperate with her.

The tiniest fringes of regret blew across her heart. He'd seemed so nice earlier, and to think it had all been an act...

Disappointment she really shouldn't feel chewed at her, lighting a fire under a righteous indignation. He deserved her anger. "You can go now. I'll speak to you when I have an attorney."

Standing near the door, Colter Blackthorn stared straight at her, his brown eyes serious but lacking the rage they'd held earlier. Something else was there now, something like regret and possibly sadness. His jaw worked slightly, probably in frustration. Finally, he pulled his phone from his pocket and glanced at it, then looked at the chair Justin had pulled up beside her bed. "May I?"

She should tell him no after the way he'd charged in here the first time, accusing her of vague crimes. But there was something about the air around him that said this time was different. It might be a tactic to get her talking, but he had her curiosity. "If you can be civil, you can sit."

His mouth twitched, and a flash of amusement skipped across his face before he could reset his stern Ranger look.

It was cute.

Before she could stop herself, Danielle rolled her eyes. Zoe was right. She needed to go on a date soon. Really soon if she was going to think the Ranger who'd just tormented her was in any way attractive. He needed to say his piece and get out the door. That was all.

Settling in the chair, Colt stared at the window across the room, his thumb tapping his phone screen, but he said nothing.

The silence stretched so thin Danielle thought she might snap in two. "Is this an interrogation tactic? Stay quiet until I talk? I've watched TV, you know. I understand how this works. I get my rights read. I get a lawyer. I get a whole lot of things you haven't given me, Mr. Blackthorn."

This time, a slow smile did lift his lips. Not a big one. Just enough to give a hint of what it would look like if he ever gave up his rigid control and let himself be fully amused by something. "Call me Colt. And you're right. I charged in here earlier and treated you worse than I should treat anyone—whether they are or aren't a criminal. You've been through a lot this evening, and I apologize."

Danielle's mouth fell open, tugging painfully at the bruise on her cheek. This was the last thing she'd expected. The man before her was contrite and humble, more like the man who'd walked into her shop and shared a moment with her about her mother. "Is it true? You lost someone?" The question popped out before she could catch it. Something in her had connected with him in that moment over her mother's statue, and she wanted it back.

His smile faded. "There are some things I won't lie about even when I'm undercover. That's one of them." The heaviness of his voice dropped it into bass territory, the tone thrumming across Danielle's heart.

Whatever meds they had pumped into her, she

needed to be off them fast. They were making her de-lusional enough to think she was attracted to this man. "Why would you have to go undercover for me? What exactly is it you think I did wrong?"

"Ms. Segovia." Colt leaned forward, his dark eyes serious. "We have a problem."

Adrenaline jolted against Danielle's chest and throbbed in the bruise on her cheek. "Whatever you think I did, I didn't. I've never—"

"It's not you." Glancing down at his cell phone and flicking through a couple of screens, he said, "Do you know who Rio Garcia is?"

Danielle's head jerked back in shock. Rio Garcia was the leader of a notorious, murderous drug cartel. Every-one in the state, maybe even in the country, knew that name. In these parts, it brought fear to most who heard it. He was known for his calculated cunning and his murderous rages, for his ability to slip away from the authorities even when they believed they had him cor-nered. She lay awake at night worrying the group her brother had gotten tangled up with was somehow tied to the cartel, because Garcia had his hands in nearly all of the criminal activity in the area. He squashed any criminal who didn't answer to him.

Her stomach roiled. This was about Justin, about his friends. This was her worst nightmare. "I don't have any connection to him."

"But the men who tried to kidnap you tonight may."

Danielle's muscles went weak. If she wasn't already lying down, she'd melt to the floor. "Why?"

Colt didn't answer the question immediately. He stared at his cell phone for what felt like an eternity, then studied Danielle's face before passing the device to her without a word.

Hand trembling, Danielle took the phone but didn't look at it. Instead, she studied the silent man beside her, trying to decide if he was friend or foe. Whatever she was holding in her hand, something told her she was about to need a friend in a very big way.

The screen went dark, and Danielle swiped her thumb to bring it back to life. At first glance, the woman staring back up at her could be her twin sister. They had the same hair, the same eyes, but the other woman had a small scar next to her ear. Still, the resemblance was enough to make her feel she'd fallen out of reality into a very bad horror movie. "Who is this?" She couldn't take her eyes from the picture. If the picture didn't include an outfit she'd never owned and a setting she'd never before seen, she'd swear the woman was her.

Colt studied her as though her reaction to what he was about to say was of vital importance. "Her name is Adriana Garcia."

Garcia. Heart pounding, Danielle stared at the woman. "She looks like me."

Holding out his hand, Colt took the phone and pocketed it. "She's Rio Garcia's sister. She's wanted by both sides of the law for multiple reasons, and both sides will do whatever it takes to get to her first."

"Why is he having to search for his own sister?" She couldn't fathom that sort of distance between siblings. "I don't understand."

"The most I can tell you is that she stole something from him, and he wants it back." He laid a hand on hers, his fingers warm as hers grew increasingly chilled. "We had intel that suggested you were her, but as you know, that intel was bad. The problem is, we believe Rio Garcia received the same intel, and that those were his men who came after you."

Danielle shook her head. Over and over again, back and forth. She wasn't hearing this. It couldn't be true.

Because if a killer like Rio Garcia believed she was the person he wanted, he would stop at nothing to drag her to him.

Over the years in the military, in police work, and in his newly minted career as a Texas Ranger, Colt had encountered his share of females in distress. While his heart normally went out to them, it always remained mostly untouched. He'd always been able to stay completely focused and professional.

When the gravity of her situation hit Danielle Segovia, draining the color from her face, his heart clinched in his chest and threatened to stop beating. It was a feeling he hadn't experienced since he was a teenager, watching as his mother suffered with the news that his brother Caleb was gone.

If he'd doubted Danielle's innocence before, there was no more question. A person could fake a lot of things, but unless they were very well trained, they couldn't make their skin pale with fear. He couldn't imagine how the news was hitting her. Learning that the leader of one of the most dangerous drug cartels in North America had you in his sights would give even the bravest man pause. The blow he'd just delivered to Danielle in the wake of her attempted abduction ought to be enough to slay her.

For the longest time, she stared at the door as though she expected it to be kicked open by Garcia's henchmen at any second. It was as though she'd forgotten Colt was there.

He squeezed her fingers, half surprised to find her hand still in his. "Ms. Segovia..."

"Danielle." Gently, she extracted her hand from his, though she didn't look at him. "What do I do now?"

Sitting back in the chair, Colt puffed out a heavy breath. This was the tricky part. With Carmen missing, the team was already short a member. He'd love to offer Danielle a twenty-four-hour guard, but he wasn't sure it was feasible, and it wasn't something he could do without Major Vance's permission. "That's up to you. We can try to locate a safe house, if you'd like."

"A safe house?" She blinked twice, and her gaze swung to him. "As in disappear?" She shook her head. "I can't do that. Justin has school. My shop can't simply shut down during our busiest time. I'm volunteering at the Mission and, this close to Christmas, they need me. And...Christmas." Her voice faded into nothing as the reality of her situation dug deeper. "Is there anything else I can do?"

Their options were limited, especially with all available resources dedicated to the hunt for Adriana Garcia. They had to keep their attention on their target. The last thing they needed was another Garcia funneling drugs into the country.

Additionally, taking down Rio Garcia had been a top priority of E Company for years and would represent a major blow to the drug trade on the US-Mexican border. He'd been on the move more than usual lately, tracking his sister. Sooner or later, he'd slip up enough for the Rangers to snap the trap. Until that occurred, they couldn't afford to lose their focus.

Except…

Colt stared at the woman in front of him. The Rangers knew Danielle wasn't Adriana, but Rio had no idea. He'd tried to take her once, and the chances were high he would come after her again. Not only was her safety as a civilian precious, but her very existence might lead Rio Garcia straight to them. She couldn't be bait—Colt would never suggest putting a civilian in danger like that—but since they knew Garcia was bold enough to try again, they might as well put someone into place to not only protect Danielle but to keep an eye out for the cartel leader's next move.

Colt was on his feet and headed for the door. He had to talk to the team, then call Major Vance. If they could have a Ranger stick close to Danielle, then Rio Garcia might play right into their hands.

"Colt?" Danielle's voice, thin and questioning, caught his ear as his hand landed on the doorknob.

He stopped. What must she think of him, practically running for the door when she'd asked him for help? "I'm sorry." He turned to her, trying to control his excitement. Adriana Garcia might have slipped through their fingers, but her brother was closer than ever. "I need to talk to my team. I have an idea about how to protect you." He probably shouldn't have said that and gotten her hopes up, but she needed to know he wasn't running out on her when she needed someone close.

Though he had no idea why he cared how she felt.

"Trust me. We'll find a way to have someone watch over you."

"And my brother."

The request jolted through Colt so hard, she had to have seen the way his head jerked. For a second, he couldn't get his voice to cooperate, the plea so close to the one his own heart had once cried. "Your— Yes. Your brother, too." He couldn't deny her that.

"Then I want you."

"Excuse me?" Colt's head tilted. "You want me for what?"

"I want you to be the one protecting Justin and me."

Colt's mouth opened then closed, no words leaking out. He couldn't be placed on a protection detail, not even if it meant catching Rio Garcia. He'd failed to be a sufficient protector in the past, when it had mattered the most. He couldn't risk another life by failing again. "I'm not... That's not my wheelhouse. I can make sure it's someone you're—"

"When my store was vandalized, I called the police. They came and did nothing other than apparently call the Rangers to tell them I was a wanted felon." The woman before him might still be weak in a hospital bed, but there was a strength in her expression and in her words that brooked no argument. Danielle Segovia was serious, and she wasn't going to back down. "It's you or nobody."

"I'll do my best." Turning his back on a request that carried the weight of history, Colt pulled the door open, then turned back to Danielle. "Why me?"

"You were sincere about my mother's memory, about the statue in my shop. You understood that. I could tell." The determination in her expression wavered and her gaze flicked to the window before resting somewhere above Colt's head. "I trust you."

The corner of Colt's eye twitched. Those were rare words. He'd never heard them from a stranger, and no one in his family had said them in years. They lay like a blanket over him, alternately warming and suffocating him. The air in the room seemed charged with something he would never be able to define.

Seldom was he at a loss for words, but everything about the moment rendered him speechless. There was no way to answer what Danielle was saying. With a curt nod, he turned and walked out the door to find his team and to attempt to convince them to give him the one job at which he was guaranteed to fail.

FIVE

Maybe it was her wild ride in the trunk of a car. Maybe it was the drugs the hospital had given her for the pain. Or maybe it was simply the absolute unreality of the whole night, but Danielle couldn't make herself open the door of Colt's car.

She'd walked out of the hospital under her own power, refusing to be wheeled out like a weak woman, but now? It was as though the world had backed away and left her empty. She simply stared down at the door, knowing she had to lift the handle, but unable to get her arm to obey.

"Let me get that for you." Reaching around her, Colt popped open the door. His chest brushed her shoulder, the warmth of him felt even through the thickness of both of their jackets.

She needed sleep. Or coffee. Maybe both. "Thank you." She slid into the car, buckled her seat belt and glanced at her phone. Still no word from Justin. He'd marched into her room a couple of hours ago, found out that Colt was going to be coming home with them, then declared her safer with the Ranger than with him. He'd left and hadn't answered his phone in the time since.

He'd better be home, sound asleep in his bed. He had school tomorrow—the last day before Christmas break—and it was already after two in the morning. With all that had happened in the past few hours, the idea of him roaming the city with his friends was almost more than she could take.

Colt got in and shut the door, resting both hands on the steering wheel but not moving to put the car into Drive. For a guy who was clearly used to taking charge and getting what he wanted from people, he'd been virtually silent since she'd demanded his protection. Other than informing her that he'd be the one standing guard at her apartment for the rest of the night, he hadn't said much else.

Clearly, something was on his mind. He'd been uncomfortable with the idea of playing bodyguard, but Danielle really didn't care. While the police officers who had worked her vandalism case had been polite, they'd failed to protect her. She didn't know any of the other Rangers well enough to invite them into her home.

Not that she knew Colt Blackthorn, either. But something in his expression when he'd mentioned losing someone had tugged at her, their broken hearts briefly speaking the same language. It wasn't much, but it was enough for her to view him as a person and not simply as an agent of the state.

Finally, he shifted the car into Drive and edged out from under the overhang at the entrance. "I can't be with you all day every day, so I'll be trading off duty with a Border Patrol agent named Kylie Perry." He kept his eyes on the road, but the flash of a grin tipped his lips before he reset his expression. "You'll like her. She's good people."

Danielle nodded, twisting the tail of her shirt between her fingers. When she'd demanded he be the man to watch over her, she hadn't considered the way it would put her into close, ongoing proximity with a stranger. Now here she sat, less than two feet between them. Should they make small talk? Was that how this worked? Or did she just keep silent and let him do his job?

In her whole life, she'd never been more uncomfortable.

Chewing her lower lip, she stared out the front window until the flicker of something high in the glass on the driver's side caught the light of a passing street lamp. She leaned forward. The telltale circular signature of a bullet impact marred the glass.

She gasped and flattened herself against the seat, her eyes widening. From her prison in the trunk, she'd been certain she'd heard gunshots, but the ramifications hadn't filtered into her mind at the time.

Someone had fired a gun at Colt Blackthorn because of her.

"Are you okay?" Colt's voice was low, laced with concern.

"They shot at you?"

He sniffed, and it sounded like an attempt to hide a low chuckle. "It comes with the job sometimes. Fortunately, like most guys who learned how to shoot by watching too many action movies, their aim was terrible."

Danielle swung her head toward him. Seriously? He was going to crack a joke when he'd been that close to death?

Colt smiled, then turned his attention back to the

road. "Don't look so surprised. This won't be the first vehicle I've returned in less than mint condition. Probably won't be the last, either." He leaned forward to inspect the top of the windshield. "At this point, I'm pretty sure my whole team would go into shock if I brought back a loaner completely undamaged."

He was so flippant about it, like it happened every day.

Maybe it did to him, but not to her. People didn't aim weapons at her, and people didn't go toe to toe with bullets, trying to rescue her. The man beside her could have died making sure Rio Garcia's men didn't get away with kidnapping her, and she'd have never known his real name.

Somehow, the thought of that brought an incredible sadness as she stared at his profile, his dark hair mussed and his jaw strong. "Thank you."

"Hey, now." He pulled his hand from the wheel and reached out to her, then stopped and jerked back with a shrug. "It's my job. I'd be a terrible Ranger if I'd taken off and done nothing."

"Yeah, but—"

"Are you hungry?"

Danielle blinked rapidly and stared at him, trying to make sense of the abrupt redirection of the conversation. "I'm... No. Are you?"

"I could use a burger. I was going to grab something after I left your place earlier but, well... Change of plans." He smiled at her again, and the look swirled in her stomach.

Maybe she was hungry after all? "Uhm, I don't have anything at the house. I was supposed to go to the grocery store when I closed up tonight, but..."

"Change of plans?" He arched his eyebrow, looking for all the world like a comedian waiting for the audience to get the joke and laugh with him.

Bless him. He was clearly trying to cheer her up, even if he was a little inept in the way he was going about it. Maybe this was that kind of sense of humor Zoe was always talking about. Danielle's closest friend had done a tour in Afghanistan before settling in El Paso to open the Mission. She'd often talked about the crazy in-jokes full of dark humor that flew around in her unit—things civilians would find morbid but that got the soldiers through their tours. Being a Ranger probably came with the same kinds of emotions.

To Danielle, bullets and death would never be funny. But she'd try for Colt since he was trying for her. "There's a diner on the corner. It's open twenty-four/ seven. Justin goes there all the time with—" she hated saying the word "—with his friends. I think it's a little too greasy, though."

"Greasy diner food at two in the morning? You're singing my song. Point me to it." He glanced at her, his smile ghosting into concern. "Or, you know what? You've had a crazy night and I'm sure you want to check on your brother. I can take you home and see if I can convince Kylie to bring me something when she drops off your car."

"It's okay. It's on the way to the apartment, just a couple of blocks away. You'll probably have to stop at the stop light across the street from it anyway." He'd done so much for her, was sacrificing something to camp out at her house tonight, she was sure. The least she could do was sit in the car while he ran in to grab a burger, although the idea of being alone, even with

Colt in full sight through the restaurant's huge glass windows, sent a shudder behind her ribs.

"It's no big deal." He seemed to sense her unease. "Kylie owes me a favor."

Danielle didn't want to feel relief, but it washed over her all the same. She wouldn't be left alone at the mercy of shadows, even for a moment.

As the car slowed at the light, she aimed a finger across the street at the diner, which was crowded with people. When the bars closed, patrons usually moved to the diners to keep the night going. "In case you decide later you…" The words died in her throat. Standing in a booth by the window, a tall teenager with his back to them waved a fan of bills, then bowed and handed them to the waitress as his friends laughed, stomping and clapping their hands.

Justin's friends, the very group she'd been trying to warn him away from. Any kid that age flashing that kind of cash in this neighborhood had earned it running drugs, she had no doubt.

As Colt pressed the gas, the car glided into the intersection, taking them right past the restaurant. "You know those guys?"

"Not personally." She started to turn away, but as they passed the huge window, the teenager dropped into his seat.

Danielle gasped, fear and anger knocking the air from her lungs.

The kid, head back and laughing, his profile in full view, was her brother.

Colt bit back a frown as he let the car coast through the intersection, watching the group of a dozen or so teenagers laugh and shove each other, slapping the back of the kid who'd obviously paid their tab.

He tasted bile and swallowed hard. Drug money. He'd pretty much guarantee it. Those guys all looked the same. They were the kind of crew Caleb had been running with as a teen, a mixture of ages, the older ones slowly gaining control of the younger, enticing them with heavy cash until they were in too deep. Whoever that young kid was, his family had better get a clue fast before the end came without warning, in a hail of gunfire.

Danielle's gasp jerked him out of the memory, and he hit the brakes, glancing in the rearview to make sure no one was behind him, then—assuming the problem must be in front of him—scanning the street to see what he'd nearly hit. "What?" He barked the word then winced. He shouldn't snap at her because of his own failures.

She didn't seem to notice he'd said anything, just stared at the front of the small diner as the waitress walked away from the table and the boys returned to their roughhousing.

All except the one closest to the window, who'd flashed the cash.

Draping his arm across the steering wheel, Colt leaned across Danielle for a better look. His jaw tightened. It was the kid from the hospital. Danielle's brother. He'd turned away from the group and was staring out the window up the street, something about his expression saying he wasn't fully in tune with the laughter of the other boys.

Ramming the car into Park in the middle of the empty intersection, Colt reached for his seat belt, instinct driving him to run into the diner and rip Justin

Segovia from the middle of that crowd before they could drag him down farther.

"What are you doing?" Danielle laid a hand on his arm.

"Going to get my…your brother." Hearing his voice ringing in his own ears, Colt sank into the seat and gripped the steering wheel with both hands. Justin wasn't his brother. Charging after the kid wasn't his job, and their family drama wasn't his business. He had his orders to protect Danielle Segovia and to keep an eye out for Rio Garcia's next move. Getting tangled up in their personal business would do nothing but distract him.

Danielle chuckled, but the sound was bitter. "When it comes to Justin, if you go in there after him, it's going to make him that much more determined to show both of us he can handle this."

"I know." *All too well.*

"I'll talk to him when he gets home." Danielle stared at her brother, fiddling with the hem of her shirt, something she'd been doing since they left the hospital. It was likely a nervous habit, one she probably didn't even realize she did. "It's just… If he's got that kind of cash, this is worse than I thought."

A lone tear glistened on her cheek in the streetlights, and she swiped it without seeming to notice. When she finally turned away from the diner, the pain etched in the lines around her mouth and across her forehead drove Colt back over a decade.

When his brother had died, Colt's heart had ached with a pain he'd tried to avoid ever since. He'd had to watch his mother grieve, had carried the weight of her pain and her condemnation before he'd run off to join the military. Right now, his own pain tore open again as Danielle's expression matched the one his mother had worn since Colt had delivered the horrible news.

His hand moved before he realized it, his fingers wrapping around hers, which were cold and trembling slightly. The only thing he knew for certain was that he had to do something, even if it was completely out of the realm of his job. "I can go in there if you want. Pull him out, put the fear of Texas law into the whole crew."

With a bitter chuckle, Danielle extracted her hand from his. "No. Justin's a quiet kid, but he'll buck like any other if you try to pin him down."

The blast of a car horn jerked Colt's attention to the rearview mirror. He'd completely lost focus, had forgotten he was sitting in the middle of an intersection. Shifting the car into gear, he took off up the street, following the route he'd traced when he'd first started trailing Danielle.

The hand that had held hers was warmer on the steering wheel, as though her touch lingered. But the farther he drove, the more the warmth turned into a burn that hardened his heart. Danielle Segovia was not his friend, no matter how much he sympathized with her plight. In a couple of weeks, this would all be over and he'd never see her or Justin again. And if he wanted her to stay alive until then, if he wanted to draw out Rio Garcia and take him down once and for all, he'd have to focus on the job, not on the tiny, broken family that had already cut into the edge of his heart.

SIX

The headlights of Colt's borrowed Challenger swept over the front of Danielle's two-story apartment building, highlighting the white wood trim that cried out for fresh paint. For the first time in a long time, Danielle really looked at the building. It wasn't the worst place in town, but it wasn't the best, either. The shop brought in enough money to cover day-to-day expenses, but she'd had to be frugal to make sure her parents' insurance money spread out enough to cover emergencies and Justin's future college expenses.

Because he was going to college, whether he liked it or not.

Of course, all of that depended on him staying out of trouble long enough to get accepted into a good school.

When Colt swung the car into a parking space directly in front of her apartment, Danielle reached for her seat belt and the door simultaneously. Ever since he'd reached for her hand outside of the diner, it seemed she could still feel Colt's touch. She needed to go inside and wash the sensation away before her overwrought and overtired mind decided she liked it. Getting attached to him on any level would be a terrible idea—even if she was dependent on him for the time being until she and Justin were safe again. It was bad enough she'd had to ride across town with him; now she'd have to find a place for him to sleep in the cramped two-bedroom apartment.

Danielle's hand rested on the handle, a stray thought nagging at her. She hadn't given Colt one direction after leaving the hospital, yet here they sat, directly below the door to her apartment. "How did you know where I live?"

Drumming his thumbs on the steering wheel, Colt gave her a sideways look before leaning forward to look up at her door. "I've been surveilling you." The statement was so matter-of-fact, Danielle nearly missed the meaning.

But when it hit, it hit full force. "You what?" Not the reaction she'd wanted to give him, but seriously?

He didn't even have the good grace to look sheepish as he turned off the engine. "My team and I have been watching you for the past few days, mapping out ways—"

"Watching me." Her voice was flat. This happened to people in movies, on cop shows. It didn't happen to her, the owner of a tiny little shop in El Paso, a woman who'd put her life on hold to raise her brother.

"Well, not you exactly. Adriana Garcia."

"Only I'm not her."

Colt opened the door and stopped with one foot in the car and one out. He turned to look over his shoulder, his expression contrite. "I forget this is all new to you. Yes, we were gathering intel on you. No, nobody was in your house or your shop."

That was good to know, but the idea that someone

had been watching her when she didn't even know it...
"Wait. Did anybody happen to see who vandalized my
shop?" Maybe, just maybe, there would be a silver lin-
ing to this.

Colt shook his head, his face tinged with regret. "No.
Your call to the police is what triggered them to no-
tify us. One of the officers believed he recognized you.
After what happened to you tonight, I think it would
be safe to say we know who did that damage." Pushing
out of the car, he stood and leaned down to look inside
at her. "I need you to hang out here for a second. Keep
the doors locked. I'm going to go check your apartment
just to make sure... Anyway, I need your keys."

She'd already handed off her car keys so one of the
Rangers could return her car, but she fished her apartment keys from the purse they had returned to her at
the hospital. Danielle passed them across the seat, then
locked the doors when Colt walked away.

She leaned forward to watch him climb the stairs.
Justin had better have put away the laundry like she'd
asked him to. She sure hadn't planned to have company
today, and definitely not a stranger like Colt Blackthorn.

When he reached her apartment, he pulled something
away from his hip, standing to the side of the door as
he opened it.

Danielle sank against the seat and pressed her fingers to her eyes. A gun. The man had just pulled a gun
to walk into her apartment. *Lord, please, please keep
us all safe.*

Safe in her own apartment. Her home. Whether
someone was in there or not, the invasion was complete. Rio Garcia's men had likely been the ones to trash

her shop. Had tried to kidnap her. Now they might have even been in her apartment.

Two taps knocked against the window.

Danielle jumped and shrieked, jerking her hands away from her eyes and whipping toward the door.

Colt backed two steps away, hands in the air and a look of horror on his face.

She couldn't help it. Between the nightmare of her kidnapping and the idea that her home may never be a sanctuary for her again, the look on Colt's face shoved her over the edge. Burying her face in her hands, she laughed until the tears rolled. It wasn't funny. Nothing about this night was even slightly amusing. But now that the dam had broken, it was either laugh or cry.

Opening the door with his keys, Colt knelt on the ground beside her. "Are you okay?"

Danielle swiped her cheeks and hauled in a deep breath. "I'm fine. It's just…" The laughter died as quickly as it had risen. "Everything is crazy."

"I know." With a quick nod, Colt stood and helped her from the car. "It's understandable."

As soon as her foot hit the bottom step in the stairwell, weariness threatened to pull her all the way to the ground. She stopped with her hand on the rail. Making it to the top was going to take all she had.

One step at a time. Just like she'd lived her whole life.

They were halfway up, Colt a few steps behind, before he spoke. "I'll see you in then come back down and bunk in the car. Lock your door and make sure—"

He wasn't staying? "I thought you were…" The heat in her cheeks was probably a glowing red indicator of her thoughts. The idea had been stupid.

"I'll be watching until Kylie shows up. She's taking

the night shift. Depending on how late you sleep, either Kylie or I will be here tomorrow, keeping an eye on things."

She nodded once. Justin had better come home soon. As the only person in the apartment, she already had a feeling sleep wasn't going to come. It would be too easy to stare at the ceiling and wait for someone to bust down the door. Once Justin got home, maybe she'd be able to catch some sleep.

Justin. Who had no job but was waving a fistful of cash.

"What?" Colt hit the top step right behind Danielle and kept pace with her to the door. "You look like something else landed on you."

Danielle lifted a smile she didn't really feel. "Just my brother. There's no telling when he'll come home."

"He usually stays out all night?"

She shrugged and pushed the door open, accepting the keys from Colt as she leaned against the doorframe. "I'm surprised he's not home tonight after..." This wasn't like him. The way he'd hovered at the hospital, Danielle had been certain he'd be a pest until she begged him to go do something else. Choosing his friends over her and leaving her alone? No, that wasn't like her brother at all.

"I'll keep an eye out for him." Colt held out a business card. "My cell's on there. Call me if you need anything. Lock the door and get some sleep." He turned and was halfway down the stairs before Danielle could convince her body to go all the way into the apartment.

She shut the door and leaned back against it, glancing around the room. Every light was on, but there were still a million places to hide. Surely Colt hadn't been able to check them all as fast as he'd been.

Resolving herself to playing hide and seek with the shadows, Danielle peeked behind the living room curtains, then headed for her bedroom to check under the bed. Get some sleep? Not tonight.

The way she was feeling now, maybe not ever again.

Climbing into the car, Colt backed into a spot that afforded him a view of Danielle's front door that wouldn't require him to crane his neck. He killed the engine and shut off the headlights, then reached for his phone as he glanced up at the apartment. A soft glow bled around the curtains. If she was at all normal, Danielle would check under every bed and in every closet, then wander the apartment all night, chasing sleep.

He'd been there. Would probably be pacing his own apartment right now if he were home. Sleep didn't come often, and usually only when he'd passed the point of exhaustion. It made him good on stakeouts, bad in every other aspect of his life.

Tonight ought to make for some good sleep then, because the evening had nearly pushed him to the edge, leaving him feeling wrecked and drained. He'd held a woman's hand. Had nearly blown everything to charge into a diner after her brother, just to give her peace and to assuage his own guilt. Even now, staring up at the dim glow from her apartment, he couldn't seem to stop thinking about the way Danielle Segovia's eyes had looked in the streetlight, the way her hand had warmed in his.

Colt whacked the back of his head against the seat a few times as though that might knock some sense into him. He'd met the woman only a few hours ago. For half of that time, he'd thought she was a drug-running murderer. His head was screwed on backward if Danielle Segovia was getting to him this way in such a short amount of time. If Austin got wind of it, there would be no end to the side jokes.

Then again, now that Austin was in love with Kylie, he'd probably sit Colt down and tell him how amazing it could be to have a woman in his life.

No, thank you. He'd let down too many people in the past. The way things were going right now, the last thing he needed to be trusting was his heart over his head.

Settling back against the seat, Colt traced the crack in the windshield with his eyes, wincing. It had grown a little since the bullet hit. Fortunately, it was a glancing blow. Still, he didn't care to hear the ribbing that was to come from the guys. He had yet to borrow a car that didn't come back with damage. Major Vance was going to start making him take a bicycle everywhere he went.

Colt grinned and dropped his head against the headrest, eyes on Danielle's apartment.

A motion on the other side of the parking lot drew his attention and pulled his spine straight.

Someone was walking up the sidewalk, mounting the stairs.

Leaning over the steering wheel for a better look, Colt traced the man's route straight up the stairs to Danielle's apartment. His feet itched to run toward the intruder, but he hesitated. It could be a night security guard or her next-door neighbor. No need to alert the world to his presence yet. If Garcia's men were watching, it could tip off the cartel and blow the whole operation.

The figure hesitated at the doorway, then turned and glanced in Colt's direction, the porch light catching the man's features.

Justin.

Colt sank against the seat and shook the adrenaline from his fingers, exhaling a breath he didn't realize he'd been holding. The young man was safe. For now. He disappeared into the apartment, shutting the door behind him.

The Segovias were all accounted for. That gave him a peace in his chest that he really shouldn't be feeling. His job was to protect Danielle. What Justin was up to was none of his business.

About ten minutes passed before Danielle's car pulled into the lot, followed by Ranger Ethan Hilliard's black pickup. Christopher Rook got out of the car and climbed into the pickup, and the two left without acknowledging Colt or giving away his position. His phone buzzed a few minutes later with a message from Rook, letting him know that Danielle's keys were under the floor mat and that Kylie would be there within the hour.

Turning the instrument lights down low, Colt found a twenty-four hour news station on satellite radio and settled in to wait. The quiet gave him too much time to think. Eventually, his thoughts turned to the new romance between his friends.

Kylie and Austin were a pair, but they'd sure been slow figuring it out. It had taken Kylie learning she was the guardian of a murdered informant's child and a hit man attempting to kill both of them before Austin had opened his eyes.

It didn't surprise Colt one bit that Valentina Hernandez had trusted Kylie enough to raise her daughter, Mercedes. Kylie was the kind of person who could make anyone feel like her best friend within thirty seconds of meeting her.

Austin was a blessed man. He'd found a woman who understood him and who made him a great match. Now, they'd be forming a family along with their adopted daughter. How long before Kylie left Border Patrol or Austin left the Rangers to pursue a safer job?

Colt puffed out a breath. He'd never let himself have a girlfriend. Sure, he'd dated off and on, but he'd never let anybody get close. The risk was too great.

Still, plenty of women had tried. Kylie said it was the whole "wounded soul" thing that did it.

That or his jawline.

He chuckled, the sound loud in the car. Whatever.

It didn't matter anyway. The job took up all of his time. Besides, loving somebody meant risking their loss or potentially letting them down when they needed him most. He'd been there, done that. It had cost him everything.

Well, that was enough of his own thoughts for one night. Punching buttons on the radio, he landed on a classic rock station and sang along, played a little air guitar… Anything to stop thinking as he kept his sights glued to the front door of a woman who had him thinking way too much about things he tried to keep locked away.

In the middle of a ballad by a band that had been popular when his parents were in high school, a shadow slipped up the sidewalk from the main road.

Colt switched off the music and straightened, watching the man walk up the sidewalk with a purpose, jacket collar up, chin tucked to his chest against the cold.

Or to hide his face.

The carefully cultivated place in Colt's gut said the guy was up to no good. He'd seen that walk too many times on men who were about to do something very, very bad.

Then again, he'd thought Danielle was one of the bad guys only a couple of hours ago. His gut wasn't to be trusted right now. Colt had to stay in place until he knew for sure something was up, or he'd reveal to the world that Danielle Segovia had the protection of the Texas Rangers.

He glanced at the apartment. The light in the window had gone out about an hour ago, and the porch light revealed nothing out of the ordinary. Nobody approached the apartment.

Yet.

This could be a distraction, though. Colt would have to work hard to watch multiple places at one time, keeping an eye on the apartment, the man and his own back.

The shadowed figure slowed his pace as he neared Danielle's car, glancing around as though checking to see if anyone was watching. He stepped off the sidewalk and disappeared beside the vehicle.

That was all Colt needed. Making sure the interior lights were shut off and the keys were out of the ignition, Colt eased the door open and crept across the parking lot, keeping his footfalls silent on the cracked asphalt. Drawing his pistol, he edged around the back of the car, ready to come up on the guy from behind. Weapon raised and ready, he side stepped around the vehicle.

No one was there.

His gaze swept the parking lot as a metal clank sounded at his feet. Before he could back up, something impacted his Achilles tendon. Pain fired up his leg, dropping him to one knee as someone under the car scrambled out the other side.

Fighting blazing pain, Colt holstered his firearm and pulled himself up, forcing a hobbled run against the agony. He only made it a few feet before a car screeched up on the road and the man jumped in.

Colt sank to the curb and jerked his phone from his pocket, gritting his teeth against the throbbing. Calling dispatch would take too long. With Kylie not in position yet, Hilliard and Rook were closer.

Ethan Hilliard answered on the first ring. "What's up?"

"I need backup at Danielle Segovia's apartment." He repeated the address. "Guy hit me and tampered with her car. Headed north in a green two-door Chevy, Texas license plate, first three J40." Propping the phone against his shoulder, he pulled off his shoe and hauled his sock off behind it, the back of his leg pulsing with every heartbeat.

"You okay?"

"Took a hit to the Achilles." He inspected the spot. No blood and, so far, no bruising. "It's going to hurt for a little while, but he didn't get me hard enough to tear anything."

"You sure?"

"Yeah. Back when I was biking I took a pedal to the back of the leg. Felt the same way. Was fine the next day. Just get out a BOLO on the car and I'll check out Danielle's vehicle. Tell anybody who responds not to blow in with their sirens and lights. I don't want her to know about this if we can help it." Killing the call, Colt slipped his shoe on and hobbled back to Danielle's car. He'd have to go home and ice the tendon, get it elevated, but experience said it would be okay tomorrow.

His conscience, however, wouldn't be. He should have been paying closer attention. Should have checked beneath the car as he approached. He'd have been able to catch the guy then for sure, before he came at Colt and caught him unaware. Chalk this up to one more mistake. The list was growing longer than he was tall.

Shoving his phone into his pocket, Colt pulled a small flashlight from inside of his jacket and knelt to peer below Danielle's car.

A wrench lay near where Colt had been standing earlier, likely the weapon that had been used against him. Farther beneath the car, a growing slick reflected the light. Dropping lower, Colt reached under the car, ran his fingers through the puddle, and sat back on his heels, rubbing his fingers together. He sniffed it to be sure.

Oil.

Whoever had crawled under Danielle's car had been trying to remove the oil plug. Drained of oil, the engine would have seized up just a couple of miles away.

Pulling himself up, Colt turned in the direction of Danielle's shop, the likely place she'd head first thing in the morning. From surveilling her over the past week, he knew she often took the back way, down some fairly low-traffic roads. If the Rangers hadn't been looking out for her and the car had seized up along one of those routes, Danielle Segovia could have vanished forever.

SEVEN

"You haven't told her?" Major Thomas Vance eyed Colt through his silver-rimmed glasses, arching an eyebrow. "What's your reasoning?"

Colt walked to the door of his boss's office, his leg tender but not as sore as he'd anticipated. He glanced up the hallway, ensuring Danielle was safely tucked away with Jenny Fielding, their resident tech guru. The two women had bonded immediately over the El Paso Rhinos hockey team and had disappeared into Jenny's office in deep discussion about Jenny's fiancé, who played right wing.

He'd grabbed a shower at home then tried in vain to grab a power nap, but he'd failed. This morning, he'd brought Danielle into the office with him. She'd argued that she needed to open the store, and he'd countered with an assertion that she had to listen to him if she wanted to remain safe.

Kylie was with Austin and Brent, processing the scene in the parking lot and having her car repaired. Danielle could have gone to work, with Kylie keeping an eye on her, but Colt felt even more responsible than ever for Danielle's safety after what he'd witnessed the night before.

He'd managed to avoid telling her about the sabotage. After the shocks she'd endured the night before, it was better to keep her in the dark about the fact that Garcia's men knew where she lived, at least until she got used to her new reality.

Scrubbing the back of his neck, he turned to the major, an imposing figure in his khaki pants, white button-down shirt and tie. Colt smoothed his hand down the front of the navy sweater he wore in place of his typical gear, since he was trying to keep a low profile. He never felt quite as put together as the rest of the Rangers in their unofficial uniform. It was different than being in the army, that was for sure.

"You plan on answering, Blackthorn?" Major Vance was a fair commander, but he didn't stand for anyone wasting his time.

"Sorry, sir. I didn't feel like she needed to know yet. She's got enough to process after learning a man like Rio Garcia is after her."

"We could put her into protective custody."

"She refuses." Colt stepped closer to the major and lowered his voice. "We can keep an eye on her as promised, which puts us in place if Garcia makes another move. Our intel says he wants his sister back pretty badly, and if he thinks Danielle is his sister—"

"He may show up in person." Sitting back in his chair, Major Vance stared at the bookshelf to his right. "It's risky, but catching Garcia would be a big deal for all of us." He whipped his gaze back to Colt. "You've got a week. If nothing happens by then, she goes into a safe house. I'm not losing another civilian." The major's expression darkened.

He had to be thinking about Valentina Hernandez, the mother of Kylie's adopted daughter. She'd paid for her invaluable help with her life, and the entire team felt the weight of her loss. Valentina's death and the subsequent attempts on Kylie's life were an added blow, coming at a time when they were already concerned with the disappearance of one of their own.

"Any word on Carmen?" As much as Colt wanted to believe Alvarez was safely in hiding, he was growing as worried as everyone else.

"Trevor Street's got a way into the lower level of Garcia's cartel. I'm sending him undercover to see what he can find out. Hopefully, he'll get a lead on Alvarez and on Garcia's sister at the same time."

Colt's stomach bottomed out. Things were worse than they appeared if Major Vance was risking another member of the Reconnaissance Team with an undercover mission now, when they had no idea under what circumstances Carmen had vanished.

"One more thing." The major pushed back his chair, indicating that this was the last thing he had to say before Colt was dismissed. "I want someone with the Segovia woman at all times. We're not taking any chances with her life or with missing Garcia when he makes a move. We've got Kylie Perry on loan from Border Patrol for the duration, and I've already told her to take the night shift. I want you on the day shift, not watching from outside but by Segovia's side at all times."

"You want me inside?" Colt stepped deeper into the room, lowering his voice. His goal here was to stay as far from Danielle as possible, not wind up next to her all day, every day. It was too close, especially the way he couldn't seem to stop thinking about her. "Is that wise?"

The major's eyebrow arched. "Are you questioning an order?"

"No, sir." Although if he'd ever wanted to do so, the time was now.

"Then you know what to do." Major Vance stood, a sure sign the conversation was over. "And Blackthorn? Leave the Challenger here. I haven't read your report yet, but I'm going to assume this one's got a few bullet holes in it like the others?"

Colt didn't answer, simply flashed a quick smile and ducked into the hallway. Now that Vance knew, it wouldn't be long before the entire company was on him about yet another vehicle damaged in a shootout. It wasn't like he went looking for trouble. Trouble just generally found him.

Outside Jenny Fielding's office, Colt stopped out of sight of the two women inside and listened to the low murmur of their voices, annoyed with himself over the way his heart rate picked up at the thought of seeing Danielle again. Right before Caleb died, Colt had been working up the nerve to ask Beth Winslow to senior prom. He'd only spoken to her a handful of times during their shared science class, but he'd been convinced she was the girl for him. The way his heart would beat faster when he saw her in the hallway, or the way he seemed to always be able to feel her sitting a few rows behind him... That was love, and it showed they were meant to be together. He'd been sure of it until she arched one perfect eyebrow at his invitation and walked away without giving him an answer.

He rolled his eyes. Same thing was happening now. This wasn't love or even intense like. He was a man, and his attention was captured by a pretty female. There were no emotions involved, just a predictable reaction to a woman whose huge brown eyes and long dark hair had probably turned more than one man's head over the years.

Colt was a stronger man than most, though, and he had a job to do. More than enough reason to ignore his heart as it revved at the sound of her laughter.

Stepping into the doorway, he spread his arms wide, faking a confidence he wasn't feeling. "You done talking about me?"

Danielle looked up and caught her lower lip between her teeth when she saw it was him.

Oh, wow. She really shouldn't do that. Now he couldn't stop staring at her lips. He should march back up the hall to Vance's office and resign. Clearly, his mind was gone.

Jenny stood, looking from Danielle to Colt and back again. As usual, her expression said she was picking up on things the average person would miss.

Well, there was nothing to see here.

But there was plenty messing with his head. The faint scent of orange and vanilla that had perfumed his car on the ride over tickled his nose yet again. Instead of closing his eyes and inhaling it the way he wanted to, he cleared his throat. "Danielle, I should get you to your shop so you can open." There was no need right now to tell her how much more of her personal space she was about to lose. That could come later, after he'd had coffee. Lots of coffee.

"So is there a reason I'm here this morning?" Danielle reached for a massive red leather purse and slung it over her shoulder, eyeing him as though she knew something wasn't right. "Mostly, I've sat in here and talked hockey with Jenny. That's not helping you catch whoever did this to me." Her fingers went to her face, where the shadow of a bruise peeked through the heavy makeup she'd caked over it.

Colt's heart squeezed. If he'd been paying attention last night, he could have saved her that bruise and the wild ride she'd taken after. Her pain was his fault.

He swallowed the guilt—along with the urge to draw her into a hug that shielded her from the world—and smiled. "Hockey, huh? With Jenny's fiancé on the team, we're headed for good things this season." He kept his face turned away from Jenny. She'd know in a heartbeat he was hiding something.

"Colt?" Sure enough, Jenny had a question.

He gave the younger woman a side-armed hug and whispered, "I've got it covered."

"Hang on there, mister." As Danielle stepped into the hallway and Colt moved to pull away, Jenny's arm snaked around his waist and held tight. She looked up at him, keeping her voice low. "I see how you look at her."

"No."

Stepping from under his arm, Jenny turned her back on the door where Danielle stood in the hallway and looked straight into Colt's eyes. "Sometimes, the harder the heart, the faster it cracks."

Colt flicked a quick glance at the hall to make sure Danielle wasn't hearing any of this. "No cracks here, Jenny." He patted her on the head. She hated when he did that. "There's not a sledgehammer big enough." Before she could say any more, he walked to the door, gestured for Danielle to go ahead of him, and kept right on walking.

The whole morning had been off the rails. Maybe it was the lack of sleep from the night before. Danielle had paced the apartment until Justin came home, then finally fell asleep with her head on the kitchen table and a cup of coffee by her elbow. She'd awakened this morning to the sound of Justin getting ready for school and Colt hammering on her door to tell her she needed to ride with him to headquarters.

He'd never given her a reason, and the lack of explanation left her feeling antsy.

She ran her hands down the leather seat of the pickup truck and gripped the edge. Instead of leading her back to the Challenger, he'd escorted her to a red extended cab four-wheel drive pickup on the far side of the parking lot. "So, they trusted you with another car? Aren't they afraid you'll bring this one back with bullet holes in it, too?"

"I thought you were too tired to remember that conversation." Colt chuckled, and the sound ran warm along Danielle's arms. "Actually, they didn't have a choice here. This one's mine. Major Vance decided if I was going to keep attracting bullets, it might as well be my personal vehicle that takes the hit."

Danielle wrapped her arms around her middle, trying to hold on to the warmth his laughter had brought. She should have guessed this truck was his. The faint smell of leather, soap and outdoors was a pretty potent blend she'd already come to recognize as belonging to

Colt Blackthorn alone. For the rest of her life, she'd associate the scent with him.

That was pretty dangerous, considering she'd only met him the night before...and he was only here because a drug lord was trying to kidnap her.

She shuddered. There were times this morning when, for just a minute, she forgot why Colt was near, that he wasn't her friend but was a Ranger protecting her from harm.

A Ranger who was keeping something from her. There was too much whispering between him and Jenny Fielding a few minutes ago. Something was up. "What was all of the hush-hush talk between you and Jenny? What are you guys not telling me? And why were you limping this morning?" She'd noticed it when he walked down the stairs, the slightest hitch in his step that wasn't there yesterday.

"Jenny likes to get involved in things that aren't always worth getting involved in. Now, let's get you to work." His tone was too practiced, the same he'd used on her the night before when he'd told her his name was Colter Beckett and he was only interested in antiquities.

"Colt, I've known you less than twenty-four hours and I already know you're not telling me the truth."

His head drew back, and a look she couldn't read flashed across his face. It could have been guilt, or maybe something softer...something scared. "My job is to protect you. I'm focused on that." His voice cracked on the words, as though he had to force them out.

She'd take any weakness she could find to get to the truth behind his smooth words. "When we left, Kylie wasn't alone in my parking lot. Two others were there with her. I recognized them from the hospital." Turning to Colt, she adjusted her seat belt and crossed her arms again, this time in a posture of defiance. "Tell me what's really going on."

"It's not what you think." He shrugged but never looked straight at her. "Last night, I found an oil leak under your car. Kylie and the others are taking care of it."

That made zero sense. "Why would the Texas Rangers and the Border Patrol care if my car has an oil leak?"

"Because we've been assigned to keep you safe. If your car leaks too much oil, your engine seizes. If your engine seizes in the middle of nowhere, then anything can happen. It's part of protecting you, Danielle." His words where tight and brusque, no room for argument.

Maybe it made a little sense. It still seemed strange, though. No movie or TV show she'd ever seen had the undercover guys doing maintenance on cars.

Unless they were secretly in love with the person they were protecting.

Danielle blushed and stared out the side window. Zoe would laugh so hard at her right now, thinking that way about a Ranger sent to keep her safe from the most notorious drug lord in the region. She'd better be careful or she'd find herself crushing on the guy simply because it was nice to feel that someone was invested in protecting her. The problem was, growing up near Fort Bliss had given her a soft spot for heroes in uniforms.

Today, even if Colt wasn't in uniform, he sure did exude the confidence of a man all geared up.

"Look…" The change in his voice made her turn her head as they coasted to a stop near the front of her shop. He was looking straight at her. "I know this is hard for you and you don't understand everything that's going on. Things that I'm used to, you're not. I'm doing my best to be sympathetic to what you're going through. Pulling a protective detail…" He curled his lip with a bitter chuckle. "It's not usually my thing. But I promise you, as long as you're with me, you're safe. I'm not going to let anything happen to you."

His voice was warm, and his gaze caught hers and held. His brown eyes softened, sweeping her face, dipping to her lips, then shifting to her eyes again. His mouth opened, then closed, his voice low, the Texan drawl thicker than normal. "I just needed you to know that."

Something about the way he was looking at her, about the way he said the words, made her want to cry, to laugh… Colt Blackthorn swamped her with an overload of emotions she couldn't process, could only drown in. That might be even more dangerous than letting a drug lord find her, because Colt wasn't here forever. He was merely doing his job, and she didn't need to be the foolish girl who turned that into something more personal.

His chin dipped to his chest, then he lifted his head and leaned closer to her. "I need to—"

A loud crack bounced through the cab of the truck as the rear window exploded behind Colt in a hail of glass and sound.

Reaching across the cab, Colt grabbed Danielle by the back of the head and shoved her face to her knees. "Stay down!" He rammed the truck into gear and blasted across the parking lot, tires squealing, the smell of burning rubber and asphalt filling the vehicle.

Tears stung Danielle's eyes where her injured cheek made contact with her knee. She tried to lift her head as

Colt took a corner, but his hand lay heavy on her back. "Don't get up." He gave a voice command to the pickup truck, and a phone rang, then Jenny's voice answered. Somehow, Colt managed to drive and keep one hand on Danielle's back, his hand running up and down her spine, reassuring her, bringing a sliver of peace she probably shouldn't feel. "Get backup over to Danielle Segovia's shop. Now. Shots fired."

"At her?" Jenny's voice sounded incredulous.

"No." Colt's hand tightened on Danielle's back for a fraction of a second. "The target was me."

EIGHT

Danielle pressed the button on the single-cup coffee-maker and leaned her head against the cabinet above it, watching the liquid trickle into her favorite red-and-green Christmas mug. If she didn't get some sleep soon, she was going to the hospital to have them install an IV line so the caffeine could skip her stomach and go straight to her veins.

"You still there, Dani?"

"Huh?" Ruffling the back of her hair, Danielle shoved away from the counter and pressed the ear bud tighter to her ear. "I'm here."

Zoe laughed softly over the phone line. "Girl, I was hoping you'd fallen asleep even though it's not even seven yet."

"I know. But sleep hasn't been my thing lately. Be-tween Justin staying out later and later and it being al-most Christmas in the retail season, then add to it…" She stuttered to a stop. Zoe couldn't know about the Rangers or the investigation—and Danielle wasn't al-lowed to tell her. That was the hard part, not being able to talk about this whole mess with her best friend. "Any-way, life can get back to normal anytime."

"When are you coming to the Mission again? The kids miss you." Zoe had founded the small Mission near the center of town over a year ago, when she'd left the military with a heart aching for the children she'd seen overseas. When she realized the extent of the poverty in her own backyard, she'd opened a center where kids could come after school and on days off to have a free meal and learn a trade. Danielle had been working with the younger children on painting crafts that she then sold in her store, donating the proceeds back to the Mission. "You haven't been in since last week."

"It's only been a week?" It felt like that long since Rio Garcia's men had tried to take her from the back of her store, and that was only last night. Struggling to cope with mountains of fear and anxiety, the night had seemed to hang on forever; then the light of day brought that strange trip to Colt's headquarters.

Then when she'd tried to go to work… Her hand shook as she reached for the coffee mug, so she laid it flat on the counter and spread her fingers wide. Someone had tried to shoot Colt Blackthorn because of her.

If he'd been hit…

Danielle sighed. That was too much to think right now.

"I heard that." As usual, Zoe was quick on the draw. "There's something you're not telling me."

There was way too much Danielle was keeping from her best friend, but there was no way to open up about it. She couldn't even dish about how Colt Blackthorn was all gorgeous and heroic—not with him standing right outside the door talking with Kylie, the Border Patrol agent who would be spending the night in Danielle's apartment.

"My coffee's ready and I've got to see about dinner." Two knocks rapped at the door, and Danielle's heart revved with them. It had to be Colt coming inside. "Gotta go. Bye." She hung up before Zoe could say another word.

Smoothing her hair, Danielle headed for the door. This was stupid. Ranger Colt Blackthorn wasn't interested in her. He was out to catch Rio Garcia and his sister. Once that happened, Colt would be gone and she'd be back to running the store by day and watching the clock while waiting for her brother to make an appearance by night.

That thought seemed a little less fulfilling than usual.

When she pulled open the door, Colt lofted two bags. "Greek samplers from Zino's?"

There he stood, tall and broad-shouldered, his brown hair tousled by the wind, a spark in his eye she hadn't noticed before. The whole picture he presented drew her in and stole her voice like the worst kind of schoolgirl crush.

His eyebrows knit together. "You don't like Greek?"

"No. I love it. Bring on the spanakopita." She forced a smile. "I was expecting Kylie to stay, is all." Close proximity with him—without anyone else there to break up the tension—might be dangerous, but it was her burden to shoulder for the foreseeable future. She'd just have to remember her place in this relationship.

"I'm going to stay a little bit later. Kylie was supposed to get some rest today, but she wound up busy dealing with...everything that happened. I sent her home for a power nap and dinner. She'll be back in a couple of hours."

After they ate, talking about everything except the

fact someone had tried to kill him earlier in the day, Danielle crushed the take-out containers into the garbage can and wiped off the kitchen counter while Colt stood in the center of the living room and stared at the curtained window.

Suddenly, she didn't know what to do in her own home. The new development of actually having a virtual stranger in her home would take some getting used to. Should she go to her room and shut the door? Stay out here and keep him company? Flop on the couch and turn on game shows like she always did after dinner? Somehow, wandering the apartment in her pj's didn't seem quite like the thing she ought to do with Colt there.

He glanced over his shoulder, his presence filling the apartment. There was something about him that exuded confidence most of the time but, right now, a shadow veiled his typical self-assurance. "Pretend I'm not here."

Yeah. Sure. That would be a piece of cake. Danielle pointed at the TV. She wasn't quite up to being alone in her room. "I usually watch TV."

"Hey, whatever you want. I'll even let you control the remote." His grin was infectious, shattering the ice between then.

"In my own living room? Thanks." Danielle aimed a finger at the end of the couch then settled into the opposite side and drew her feet up beneath her. If there had been another chair in the room, she'd have taken it, but she and Justin had gotten by with the old couch from their parents' house for so long, and no other furniture would really fit into the cramped living room.

Colt swiped the remote from the end table and held it out to her. "I have no idea what's on."

Danielle waved it off. "To be honest, I don't really

think I want the noise tonight. My brain's on overdrive already."

"You want me to be somewhere else?" Colt slid to the edge of the couch and moved to stand, glancing around the tiny apartment. "This is intrusive, I know, so maybe—"

"No." Danielle reached for his hand. If he left, she'd be alone, haunting the front window, watching for her brother. Not to mention, the quiet would fill with the sounds of gunshots and false images of Colt being hit, injured or even dead because of her. Throughout the daylight hours she'd fought those images, wounding her heart deeper every moment. In the dark? She was pretty sure a bloody Colt would haunt her. "Stay. It's really okay."

He settled into the seat again, watching her warily.

Probably because she was still holding his hand. Jerking away, Danielle crossed her arms and laid her head on the back of the couch, watching the lights on the Christmas tree in the corner brighten and then fade in a random pattern, bathing the room in a festive glow she didn't feel. The Christmas spirit wasn't hitting her this year. This was usually her favorite time of year, buying presents, seeing so many reminders of her Savior's birth. But this year? So much was happening. She hadn't even been able to buy Justin's gift yet, wasn't even sure what to get for him.

She glanced at the clock on the kitchen stove. Nearly nine. According to Colt, Kylie would be here any minute, but it would be at least a couple of hours before Justin got home, full of excuses and brush-offs.

"It's your brother, isn't it?" Colt turned, one foot on

the floor and one leg bent on the couch between them. "You're worried about him."

"I am." Danielle drew her lower lip between her teeth. She hadn't confessed her full concerns to anybody, not even Zoe. Last night with Colt, when they'd seen Justin in the diner, instinct had told her she could trust him with the truth about her brother. Now that he'd asked, the words came out of their own volition. "Justin's a good kid."

"I know." The low rumble of his voice ran across her skin and into her stomach.

Maybe it was the exhaustion. Maybe it was having another adult to talk to. His understanding brought an ache to her throat, breaking down the last of her resistance. "Our parents were killed on I-10 five years ago. Big pileup. Justin was just a kid. I was in college, working on my business degree..." The phone call had been awful, the worst moment of her life. She'd just started her sophomore year, was excited about her classes and landing a spot in a great dorm on campus... Was still so much a kid herself. Then the call came during a dorm meeting, bringing her entire world down on her head.

"You gave everything up to take care of him."

Danielle nodded once, then shifted in her seat and rested her head on the couch, facing Colt. "At first, I worked retail during the day. Finished up classes in night school while my friend Zoe watched Justin. Saved every penny I could, plus what was left from the insurance money, and finally opened the shop about a year ago." It had been a struggle to bring it all together, but one so worth it. She'd been able to preserve and protect the art so important to her mother's heritage. "A few months ago, Justin heard me complain to Zoe that some months it was a struggle to make ends meet. He started coming home with money. Twenty bucks here, fifteen there—said it was from odd jobs."

"When did you figure out the truth?" Colt's voice was tight, and his jaw stiffened as he stared at something behind her in the kitchen. There was more to the question. Danielle just couldn't figure out what it was. He had a way of growing pensive every time Justin's name came up, as though her worries bled into him.

"A few weeks ago, not long before the shop was vandalized, he came home with a wad of cash. Then last night, seeing him with all that money at the diner..." Danielle shrugged and tried to shake off the fear. "Colt, what do I do? He's fifteen. He's too big for me to control." Shoving up from the couch, Danielle walked to the tree, lifting an ornament Justin had made only last year. The painted cross was an art project she'd done with the children at the Mission, and he'd come along, helping the younger kids, laughing with them, still so much a kid himself. One year later, he'd somehow morphed into a young man she hardly knew. "All I know to do is pray, and I do that all of the time."

Behind her, Colt made a sound that sounded almost derisive, as though he dismissed the idea.

He could think what he wanted. Her Savior was the only lifeline she had, the one that had sustained her every step of her life.

The one Justin seemed to have turned his back on.

She swiped at a tear and wrapped her arms around herself. What would life be like right now if her parents had lived? For one thing, she knew she wouldn't be standing here, facing a Christmas tree with no spirit, suffering alone. "Know what I want for Christmas? My brother back. The way he was. Safe."

There was a rustle, then a warm hand rested on her shoulder, turning her slightly.

Colt tilted his head down so that he caught her gaze, his eyes filled with something Danielle couldn't read, something like understanding, something that drew her in and made her want to drown in him. "Justin will be okay." He tucked a lock of her hair behind her ear, then lifted her chin with his finger. "I will do everything in my power to make sure of that."

The low rumble of his voice in his chest, that intense look in his eye, deepening the hot chocolate color to something even warmer, caught Danielle's next breath and lodged it in her throat. His hand on her shoulder was enough to weaken every muscle in her body.

His eyes hooded, dipping to her lips.

She could melt into him right now and let the rest of the world vanish, let his arms hold her up, let his lips…

Three light raps on the door splintered the connection.

With a start, Colt pulled his hands away and held them up and to the sides, like a man surrendering. He took a step back, glanced at the front door, then at the TV. "I…" His hands fell, smacking against his jeans with a dull slap. He shook his head and cast her a look of regret, like he had more to say but couldn't find the words. "Kylie's here. I have to…to go." With one last glance in her direction, Colt grabbed his leather jacket from the kitchen chair, strode to the door and disappeared into the cold evening.

Resting his head against the back of the seat of yet another borrowed vehicle, Colt slid low and stared out the windshield at the diner, where the crew Justin Segovia had been with the night before once again sprawled in what must be their customary booths. The rowdiness seemed a bit more subdued than the night before. They were heading out soon by the way they were behaving.

Justin was nowhere in sight. Hopefully he'd already headed back to the apartment. Colt should have headed straight home and tried to get some rest, but he couldn't do it without checking on Justin for Danielle.

Colt dragged his palms down his cheeks. Danielle. How stupid could he be? He'd almost kissed her. Had wanted to kiss her.

Man, had he ever wanted to kiss her.

One minute, she was talking about her brother and he was thinking he should comfort her, tell her it was going to be okay, maybe share a little bit of his story. That urge had been bad enough. But then she'd turned and faced him and those eyes… Those big, dark eyes full of pain and sadness after her story of sacrifice and love… *Know what I want for Christmas? My brother back. The way he was. Safe.*

Something in his heart had given way. More than comfort her, he'd wanted to pull her close, tell her she was valuable, that someone understood and appreciated her sacrifice. That someone cared.

That *he* cared. He cared with a blazing ache that seemed to burn right through every ounce of common sense and professional detachment he'd ever had.

The warmth of her cheek was still on his palm. He scrubbed his hands against his jeans, trying to burn away the sensation of smooth skin and salty tears.

What was wrong with him? She was a virtual stranger. Part of an active investigation. He was smarter than this. Stronger than this. He was part of a larger group keeping an eye on her, a cog in the wheel, not her personal bodyguard.

Not her sworn protector.

He should march into Major Vance's office tomorrow and pull himself from this detail. Being attracted to a woman he was supposed to be protecting was foolishness. It was the kind of thing that happened in sappy chick flicks.

A flurry of motion across the street jerked him out of his self-condemnation. Half a dozen of Justin's friends pushed out the door, following an older man who was clearly leading them. Instead of heading toward the parking lot, they walked up the street, hands stuffed in pockets, the joking air from the night before gone.

Whatever was going down, it was all business.

Thankfully, Justin wasn't with them. If things went his way tonight, Colt might be able to catch the whole crew in the act of something illegal—moving drugs or shuttling stolen property—so he could call in the cops and have the group taken down while Justin was away. That might wake him up and see that easy money was usually a dangerous thing.

Tailing them in the car would be too risky, so Colt zipped his jacket high, tucked his chin into the collar, and followed on foot.

At the corner, the group took a right onto Mesa Verde Street. Colt followed at a distance until they all turned onto the sidewalk of a house. Crossing to the other side of the street, Colt kept his head down and walked by, keeping one eye on the front of the house. It was an older stucco home, and one that twanged against his mind with a particular familiarity.

Mesa Verde Street. This house. He'd seen it before. Colt pressed his lips together. Peter Sullivan.

Colt should have recognized that bleached blond hair immediately. A Brit with drug possession and assault charges decorating his extensive record, "Limey Pete" had been known to harbor members of the Garcia cartel. In fact, Kylie had been abducted from this very street by Miguel Ibarra, a low-level runner for Garcia.

If Justin was in with these guys, he was in something deeper than Danielle feared. This was a small part of a much bigger, deadlier operation.

So much like Caleb. The back of Colt's neck heated, frustration and renewed grief warring inside him. His baby brother had had his head turned by the promise of quick cash. He'd jumped in with all he had and had paid for it with his life.

Keeping his chin tucked to his chest, Colt walked on, trying to avoid lingering in a way that would draw attention. There was nothing he could do tonight. DEA, Border Patrol and the Rangers already had the house on their radar. Although he'd like to go in with his badge and his gun at the ready, bravado would only get him killed.

Hanging a left up the next street to double back to his borrowed car, Colt stared up at the sky, only a few stars visible above the lights of El Paso. There had to be a way to get Justin Segovia away from Peter Sullivan before the kid got in any deeper, or before Limey Pete figured out Justin was connected to the woman Garcia believed was his sister.

In the car, he cranked up the heat and drove the few miles to Danielle's apartment, unable to keep from checking on her one last time. The complex wasn't exactly in the best neighborhood, but it also wasn't one with a lot of major crime. She'd done well for herself and Justin. The inside of the place was comfortable and warm, exuding the kind of feeling that spoke of family dinners and home.

His own apartment was the opposite. Undecorated and grim, with little furniture aside from a recliner in front of a television that sat on a glass and metal stand. A bed and dresser in his room. Colt rolled his eyes. He didn't even have a kitchen table, instead eating take-out meals in front of the TV. Going home was never a joy. It was a place to rest and fuel up for the next day's work.

Maybe that was the reason for the restlessness he'd been feeling lately. It could also be why he'd nearly made a fool of himself by kissing Danielle. It could be that he finally wanted to settle down and to find a place to call home. That was a thing, right? Kylie had called it nesting. Did men ever do that?

When this was all over, maybe he could hire somebody to come in and make his apartment feel more like Danielle's did.

Except there still wouldn't be anyone there to come home to at the end of the day.

Gripping the steering wheel, Colt turned into the parking lot of Danielle's apartment complex. Hopefully Justin was home and Danielle would be able to get some rest.

He shifted the car into Park and killed the engine as a figure on the sidewalk passed under the weak streetlight.

Justin.

For once, he was alone.

Maybe Colt couldn't be close to Danielle, but he could try to talk some sense into Justin. Shoving out of the car, Colt jogged across the parking lot toward the boy.

Justin whirled toward him at the sound of the footsteps, his hand going to his hip before he realized who Colt was and relaxed.

The move caught Colt's nerves and hung there. That reflexive motion was usually reserved for people who were packing something other than their cell phones. If the move was that habitual and instinctive, then Justin was further gone that Colt had realized.

As much as Colt wanted to have it out with Justin right here and now, he had to play this just right or he'd lose Danielle's brother the same way he'd lost his own.

The thought burned his throat and stiffened his muscles with fear. He couldn't let that happen, not on his watch. Justin Segovia had to see the truth.

Right now, the kid was eyeing Colt and the stairs to his apartment, as though ready to make a fast getaway. "Ranger Blackthorn. Is my sister okay?"

"Danielle's fine. Worried about you." Colt made a show of glancing at his watch. "She'll be glad you're home at a decent hour."

"Are you about to start in on me, too? I told her. My friends are good people. They're helping us out."

"Really." Colt couldn't keep the venom from his voice. This conversation, that slight defiance in Justin's posture... Caleb had said those exact words, had stood that exact way. The fear that he'd look Justin in the eye and see his own brother nearly brought Colt to his knees.

He swallowed the emotion. "Helping you out how?" The echo of his own words from a decade ago. How was he here again?

"I run a few errands, I get paid. I get paid and Dani worries less about the rent." A sudden defiance drew Justin's shoulders back, and he took a step toward Colt. "I take care of my sister. That's all I do. She took care of me, now I'm returning the favor."

Colt pulled himself to his tallest, putting him a couple of inches above Justin. Two could play this game. Four years in the military had taught Colt how to stand taller than the man opposing him, even if the height advantage wasn't in his favor. Against a fifteen-year-old? The boy didn't stand a chance. "Justin, hear me clearly. Those guys? They're not your friends. Trust me. They're only looking out for you long enough for you to—"

"Whatever, man." Justin backed up and held out both hands out to his sides, defiance replaced with the kind of impudence only a teenager could throw. "You don't know my sister or me, so just do your job. My sister's your business, not me."

Pivoting on his heel, Justin stalked up the stairs, slamming the apartment door behind him.

Colt headed toward the stairs but stopped with his hand on the rail, his head hanging, grief and anger a toxic blend in his gut. The words were a wake-up call from a fifteen-year-old kid. Justin was right. Colt had no authority or right to interfere with the boy. Colt had a job to do, and it wasn't getting personally involved with the Segovias.

It certainly wasn't saving Justin. Colt couldn't do it. He'd failed his own brother. What if he tried to save

Danielle's brother and failed again? No way could he handle it if Justin died in his arms the way Caleb had.

No, he had to back away in order to protect the Segovias…and himself.

NINE

As they walked up the hallway of Echo Company headquarters, Colt couldn't find a word to say. Major Vance had called an "all hands" briefing. Something big had to be on the horizon, and the possibilities wouldn't stop spinning in his head.

Beside him, Danielle fingered the strap of her huge purse, twisting it as their footsteps echoed up the hallway to Jenny's office. "I'm sorry to keep dropping you off with Jenny."

"I understand. It's just…" She shrugged.

"Just what?" Sorting out his own mind was impossible, but he could be here for her. Technically, it went beyond the bounds of his job, but she needed more than someone to shield her from a formidable enemy. Besides, he needed her thinking clearly and in her right mind if the danger ever drew closer.

Her smile was half-hearted. "Nothing."

Colt wanted to turn her toward him, put his hands on her shoulders and let her know she could tell him anything. But that would come too close to what had almost happened between them the evening before and he had to maintain distance. Still… "You never know. Rang-

ers are capable of handling anything. We're trained."
He forced amusement into his voice.

Her smile flickered, then faded. "I'm having to keep
the store closed. It's Christmas, the busy season…" Her
shoulder edged upward again. "That's not your problem."

Somehow, Colt felt as though it was. He could make
her no promises, but he'd get that store open for her tomorrow, even if he had to staff it himself. The Garcia
family had already cost Danielle so much. He wouldn't
let them steal her livelihood, as well. "We'll figure
something out."

At Jenny's door, the younger woman made a fuss
over Danielle and the pair walked away without acknowledging Colt. He watched them for a moment,
missing the ease between Danielle and him, although
this was for the better.

Even if it felt all wrong.

Colt dropped into a seat in the briefing room and
stared at the bank of screens at the front. The jokes
about his truck were coming, no doubt, and he'd have
to deal with it.

Usually, joking around with his team was easy and
fun, but that bullet yesterday had narrowly missed him,
and it could have hit Danielle. One more weight added
to an already heavy burden.

Ford Manning strode into the room, changed direction when he saw Colt and leaned against the metal
table. "So… Had any friendly chats with your insurance
agent lately? What's the deductible for a bullet strike?"

Colt sat back and crossed his arms over his chest.
"You've had all night and half of today and that's the
best you could do?"

Dropping into the seat next to him, Ethan Hilliard cut off whatever Ford was planning to say. "Don't ask to borrow my car. I like my paint job. I'm pretty fond of my back window, too."

Colt sucked his teeth and nodded. "I'm fine—thanks for asking. Didn't even get nicked."

Ford slapped him on the back of the head, then got up and walked to another table to sit down. "Cool your jets, Blackthorn. If you weren't okay, we'd all be fighting over who got to keep your truck instead of harassing you."

"Count me out. I haven't got the money for the repairs." Ethan grinned and made a show of shoving his keys out of Colt's reach. "Whose car are you driving today, and are they aware of the consequences?"

Before Colt could respond, a no-nonsense voice cut in from the back of the room. "If you're done hassling Blackthorn, I'd like to get down to business." Major Vance's voice silenced the ribbing as his footfalls thudded up the aisle. The rest of the Rangers took their places at various tables around the room. "Just so we're all clear, I gave Blackthorn a bicycle. Makes a smaller target."

As the chuckles around the room died, Colt nodded with a tight smile. "If y'all would quit calling me to save you, there'd be a lot fewer cars in the scrap heap." He tried to laugh with them, but it was tough. Having Danielle in the truck when the bullet hit was too close for comfort.

"You're a hero to us all." Major Vance leaned against the table at the front of the room and crossed his arms, his forearms resting on the Texas-sized belt buckle at his waist.

Colt glanced around. Trying to maintain a low profile while he kept an eye on Danielle, he was the only Ranger out of the unofficial uniform. Other than his boots, he could pass for any guy on the streets. Sure, Kylie had on civilian clothes, but she was on loan from Border Patrol. It was a wonder no one had called him on being out of uniform on top of the new bullet holes.

"I called y'all in because I wanted to update you. According to Blackthorn, Peter Sullivan's back in the picture. DEA has eyes on his house, watching to see if Garcia makes an appearance. On top of that, McCord's received another message."

Every head in the room turned toward Brent Mc-Cord.

Colt's jaw tightened. Normally, Brent would be in the chair beside him, but the man he'd formerly counted as a friend was as far across the room as he could get.

Casting a frosty glance at Colt, Brent walked to the front, stopping to type on the main computer. "As you know, someone sent a letter to me here. It was postmarked El Paso and said Adriana Garcia is somewhere on the Rio Grande." The big screen came to life, with the image of a handwritten note. *Adriana loves llamas.* "This one came in today."

Colt exhaled loudly before he could catch himself.

Brent turned toward him. "You have something to say?"

What he was thinking was not fit to be shared publicly, but Brent likely wouldn't back down unless Colt answered. "*Adriana loves llamas?* It sounds like something a child would write."

"Handwriting and textual analysis says we're dealing with a teenager who isn't a native speaker." Brent turned, dismissing Colt. "It could be an informant or someone acting on behalf of Adriana herself."

"Why would she send you notes?" This time the challenge came from Ford. "If she wants to turn herself in, why be cryptic?"

Brent shook his head, eyes on the screen. "She can't show her face around here. It's clear someone in Garcia's organization is watching us, riding our coattails while we look for her. The minute our eyes were trained on Danielle Segovia, there they were. Maybe this is her way of keeping out of her brother's line of sight while asking for help."

"Or she's guilty and knows that only you would ever believe otherwise." Colt couldn't listen anymore. Brent had to see this blind devotion to a woman he'd met once bordered on insanity. Too much evidence pointed to her stealing her brother's drugs and money to seed her own organization.

Ethan elbowed him and gave him a sharp look. Everyone else ignored him.

From his spot at the front, Major Vance retook command. "We also got DNA results on the scarf used to kill Agent Gunn. We can say with about eighty-five percent certainty it belonged to Adriana Garcia."

For a heartbeat, Brent froze at the front of the room, then he turned and walked out.

When Major Vance jerked his head toward the door, Ford followed.

Colt slapped his hand on the table. "So we're definitely after her for Greg's murder?"

"The evidence is stacking up." Major Vance scratched his chin. "We'll do our best to find her, bring her in, and go from there. Guilt or innocence isn't for us to decide."

His eyes swept the room, hesitating on Colt. "We'd all do well to remember that."

Easy for Vance to say. It wasn't his best friend who'd betrayed them, who had sold out his country for cash. It wasn't his best friend lying six feet under because a thieving killer had turned her fury on him.

"We'll keep our eye on these messages but we won't put any man hours into them. They're too cryptic to know if they're real. Could be a prank or a trap. If McCord gets more, we'll update everyone, but nobody's going out on the Rio Grande hunting llamas."

No one chuckled. It may have sounded like a joke, but it wasn't. Thomas Vance had already made his one wisecrack for the day. Adriana Garcia was serious business.

Brent and Ford slipped back into the room and took their seats. The lines around Brent's mouth were tight, his jaw set.

Colt wanted to offer him something, but he had no idea what Brent needed. At one time, they'd have grabbed some pizza, watched the game and worked through this. Adriana Garcia had driven a wedge between them, with Brent blind to everything but the big brown eyes that he claimed held innocence.

Killing the image on the screen, the major glanced at his cell phone, then laid it on the table. "None of that is the reason you're here. Trevor Street contacted me." He held up a hand to stem the inevitable question. "No word on Alvarez."

There was a collective exhale of frustration. The longer Carmen was silent, the more likely she was in serious trouble.

From the back of the room where he sat with Kylie,

Austin called out, "She's smart enough to stay hidden if the heat's on her."

Colt nodded. He'd trained with Carmen. She was street-smart, tough…

"We'll keep an eye out for her. She's priority one. But Garcia knows we're up to something. He's put a gag order on his men. They're not to trust anyone outside of the organization. Fortunately, because Street was undercover with this group before, they consider him an insider and gave him information."

Something in the major's tone pulled Colt straighter. Things were about to break wide open, no doubt.

Major Vance pulled off his silver glasses and laid them on the table, a sure sign things were intense. "Garcia's trying to replace the drugs his sister stole. He has a major cash flow problem and he's looking to rebuild the coffers fast. He's got a shipment crossing the border at Tornillo in just over forty-eight hours. We're coordinating with Border Patrol and DEA." He turned toward Kylie. "Agent Perry, I'm pulling you off the Segovia protective detail. Your chain of command requested you back with them since you've worked the area before."

Balling his fist on the table, Colt waited. This was a huge opportunity. An operation this size would recall every man to his station. This mission might be the thing that tore him away from Danielle and forced him to focus on what he was meant to do. Not bodyguard duty, but hitting the field and taking down bad guys.

"Blackthorn—" Vance's gaze swung to Colt "—you're on your own with Ms. Segovia. Garcia's men could hit her at any time. We're arranging backup with El Paso PD."

Wait. He was being banned from the mission? His team was about to gear up without him? "Sir…"

Vance grabbed his phone and pocketed it without looking at Colt. "I need you where you are." He turned to the rest of the team. "Grab your gear and meet here in two hours." He was out the door before Colt could make his case.

As the rest of the team flowed out of the room, Colt stared at his fist on the table. He'd suspected it, but the evidence was undeniable.

His failure to see Greg for the traitor he'd become… His misstep in identifying Danielle Segovia as Adriana Garcia… No one could trust him to get it right on one of the biggest missions they had ever undertaken.

His team had lost faith in him.

TEN

Pulling her hair back in a ponytail and securing it with a hair band from her wrist, Danielle walked behind the row of children seated at long wooden tables in the Mission's main room. Fourteen wiggly bodies, antsy to get at the paint and ornaments in front of them, practically danced in their seats.

Normally, working with the kids let her leave all of her troubles at the door. Their giggles and grins were the antidote for every problem.

Today, one particular problem continued to dog her. Colt paced the room, watching everything. Since his meeting at headquarters this morning, he'd grown more distant and quiet. The only time he'd truly focused on her had been to fight her on coming to the Mission this afternoon.

The truth was, her head kept telling her this was stupid. She was in danger. Her presence might endanger the kids, as well.

But a frantic call from Zoe had pushed her into this. A routine dental visit had turned into oral surgery, putting Zoe out of commission. The other afternoon volunteer was sidelined with a stomach virus, and her backup was visiting family in Arizona.

The Mission couldn't open without Danielle's presence, and if the doors stayed closed, the children would have nowhere to go after this last half day of school before the holidays, which meant that either they'd fend for themselves or parents would have to give up income to leave their jobs early.

Saying no without an explanation would have raised a whole slew of questions Colt had insisted Danielle couldn't answer, in addition to leaving the children vulnerable on the street.

Finally, Colt had given his reluctant agreement, but only on the condition that he'd be inside with her, and an El Paso police officer would watch the front parking lot. Danielle should feel safer, but she couldn't stop thinking of the worst possible scenarios. Forcing a smile to her face, she tried to focus on the children who needed her.

Danielle stopped to give a genuine smile to Justin who, along with three of the older children, was doing his best to corral the youngest into submission. He'd been his old self today. After coming in at a decent hour last night, he'd chatted with Kylie for a little while and then disappeared to bed. Today, he'd offered to come to the Mission with her.

It was like old times.

Except old times hadn't included a Texas Ranger standing silently in the corner.

Danielle glanced over her shoulder. Colt stood in the doorway, hands shoved into the pockets of his jeans, a deep red button-down shirt doing everything to bring out the color of his eyes and enhance the dark of his hair. He looked amazing.

And entirely too serious.

Clearly, last night had affected him. When he'd taken over for Kylie this morning, he'd been reserved and silent, speaking only four words. "Good morning" when he came in the door and "thank you" when she offered him a cup of coffee. He'd stayed at the front window of the store this morning, alternately watching the parking lot and talking on his cell phone until the call came that forced her to close the shop and rush to headquarters with him.

If she were choosing a word to describe him today, it would be *cold*. Gone was the man who had laughed at the bullet holes in his car, had brought her dinner, had sympathized over her plight with her brother...had nearly kissed her.

Maybe he was embarrassed because he'd thought she'd thrown herself at him. She hadn't, had she? Wrinkling her brow, Danielle tried to remember how last night's conversation had gone down, but all she could picture was Colt's eyes dipping to her lips as though he'd wanted that kiss as much as she had.

Even now, the memory made her knees weak enough to grab the back of a chair and glance toward Colt again.

He was looking straight at her.

The lines of his face were tight and all business, but something in his eyes softened when they caught hers.

He turned away, staring at the front door instead.

Well, that was that. She could put a pin in the fantasy she hadn't wanted to acknowledge...that a man like Colt Blackthorn could be interested in a woman like her.

It was probably better he'd backed away. His *harrumph* at her mention of prayer the night before had niggled all day at the back of her mind. Her faith was everything to her, and if he derided that, well… She sure wasn't into missionary dating.

"Dani?" Justin's voice drew her attention back to the table, where fourteen expectant faces watched her. "I think they're ready to paint."

Determined to forget Colt Blackthorn's existence, even as his eyes practically burned holes in the back of her shirt, Danielle clapped her hands together. "Everybody remember the instructions?"

"Yes!" The chorus of shouts was deafening. They were for sure ready to be set loose with brushes and poster paint, although their enthusiasm might result in more messes than masterpieces.

"Okay, then. Listen to your big kid helpers and do your very best. I'll put the ornaments you paint in my shop and all of the money will come back here to buy more fun stuff for you to do. Sound like a plan?"

The kids cheered and dove in. The girls tended to be methodical, choosing colors carefully and holding their brushes to paint meticulous strokes along the lines. The boys?

Danielle bit back a grin. Well, they tended to be more creative.

A female laugh behind her turned her toward the door and Colt.

He wasn't alone anymore. Kylie had appeared, and Danielle turned just in time to see her laugh at something Colt said.

His smile lit his entire face in a way Danielle had yet to experience directed toward her. He was twice as gorgeous when he smiled, and laughter eased the tight lines of his face.

The butterflies in her stomach crashed into the pit.

That smile was for Kylie, who clearly brought him a joy Danielle couldn't match.

That was probably why he'd been so cold today. There was something between him and Kylie, and Danielle had misread the entire situation, had thrown out crazy signals to a man who had already given his heart away.

It made sense. They worked closely together and probably saw each other all of the time. Kylie seemed to make Colt happy.

Which did nothing to ease the green sting of envy that caught Danielle somewhere in the center of her chest. Turning away before they could catch her staring, she leaned over little Matteo's shoulder and tried to force her attention to his work. "That's a beautiful snowflake you're painting."

"*Gracias*, Danielle." He smiled up at her with a gap-toothed grin, then went back to work.

"Why choose red for a snowflake, though?" Those boys…creative for sure.

"*Rojo* is my favorite color."

"No better reason than that." She patted him on the head and straightened, glancing over her shoulder. Kylie had vanished, and Colt stood staring at something across the room, a scowl darkening his expression. Other than the moment with Kylie, she hadn't seen him truly smile all day.

She turned back to the table. *Danielle, you're a fool.* The truth cut. Sharply.

An elbow to her ribs jerked her upright. Colt?

When she turned, it was her brother, eyeing her with a questioning expression. "What's wrong with you?"

His voice was low enough to carry to her while keeping the giggling children isolated from the conversation.

"Plenty and you know it." She moved on to look over Olivia's work, then started to slip around the table, but Justin caught her by the elbow.

"Dani, I know you're worried about everything that's going on." He drew her away from the table. "If you listened to me and put a gun in the shop, and if you'd let me—"

"I already told you no." She gently pulled her elbow from her brother's grasp and turned to face him, keeping her voice low. "That's asking for trouble, and you're not old enough anyway."

Anger flashed in his eyes. "So the Rangers are going to follow you around forever?"

"For the moment, yes." She was not having this conversation now. In fact, not ever again. "As for you having a gun, the answer remains a firm no. You turn eighteen, you can do what you want, *hermanito*. Until then, absolutely not. There are too many ways for you to get into trouble."

"I'm careful."

"Other people don't know that." Danielle pressed her fingertips to her temples. "You mean well. I get it. But let me handle the big stuff. You worry about being a kid. Colt and Kylie are all we need right now."

"Kylie. I saw her a few minutes ago. Will she keep hanging around for a while?" Justin turned toward the kids, keeping his face away from Danielle, though his ears pinked slightly.

Danielle bit back a chuckle. So that was why he'd come home early and sat around the living room talking last night. The petite Border Patrol agent had caught his eye. "She's more than a decade older than you."

"Did I say anything?"

Danielle flicked his ear. "You didn't have to."

Her amusement faded quickly, though. Like sister, like brother...both wanting what they couldn't have. "Hey, how about after we leave here, you and—"

A sharp whistle cut the air, silencing the children's voices and giggles.

Danielle whipped toward the sound. Three older teenagers stood at the front door, their expressions dark. Wearing jeans and oversized T-shirts, their arms sporting multiple intricate tattoos, they were the textbook picture of trouble. And they were watching her brother expectantly, clearly waiting for him to rush to their side.

The kids looked at them and quickly turned back to their painting, probably used to seeing that type running the streets around their homes.

Justin brushed past her, headed for the door.

Wait. No. He wasn't leaving with them. He couldn't. Whirling toward Colt, Danielle sent him a panicked, silent cry for help, but he was already in motion, headed for the group who eyed him with dark suspicion.

Danielle grabbed her brother's shirt and held him back. "Where are you going? I..." She couldn't exactly order him to stay. He'd rebel, try to save face in front of his so-called friends. "I need you here to help finish."

Extracting himself from her grasp, he turned to look at her, then glanced back at the young men who were now talking in harsh whispers with Colt. "Can't stay. I have someplace to be."

"Justin..." She hated the pleading in her voice. She

was his guardian, his sister. He should know she only wanted him to be safe.

But he was also her brother, and whatever he was involved in, it was bigger than her and downright terrifying.

Breaking away from the group at the door, Colt took carefully measured steps toward Justin, undoubtedly trying to appear casual in front of the children. After a quick, heated discussion, Justin stepped around Colt, who stared after him with a mixture of grief and frustration. He finally looked at Danielle and shook his head once.

She knew what that look meant. He couldn't stop Justin from leaving. There was no legal reason to detain him, no recourse short of sheer force that would only escalate the situation and perhaps put the children in danger.

Fourteen small faces stared up at her, and they would undoubtedly feed off of what she did next. Pasting a smile on her face, she gestured for them to get back to work, then turned to watch Justin walk away.

He stopped halfway up the aisle and turned to her, a small smile on his face. "Trust me, Dani, I'm okay. These guys? They'll take care of me. Of us. Even after the Rangers are gone."

Ruffling Matteo's hair as he passed, Justin joined the group at the door and filtered out behind them, disappearing into the hallway and ripping Danielle's heart out with every step.

"*Adios*, Matteo!" Danielle tossed a bright smile to the young boy, who waved with one hand while clinging tightly to his sister's with the other.

She closed and locked the double doors and leaned her head against the cool wood. The time since Justin left had been the longest three hours of her life, but the children were all safely on their way home. Today had dragged on for an eternity. She was done. Ready to go home, put on her pajamas…

Except she couldn't. She was still under the watchful eye of Colter Blackthorn and, although he'd stepped out into the parking lot to watch as the children left, there was no doubt he'd be inside shortly to keep a direct eye on her. After all, duty called, and he wasn't the type to turn his back on his job.

His job. The words sank her heart. That was all she was. All she could ever be. Somehow, every time she looked at him, that was a fact she managed to forget.

It was a fact she'd do well to remember. Whether Colt was interested or not, it definitely appeared he was spoken for.

Not that Danielle cared.

Except she did.

Waving her hand in front of her face, Danielle turned toward the room, planting her hands on her hips. No more thoughts wasted on Colt Blackthorn and his amazing brown eyes. All it did was drag her down. With Christmas coming quickly, she needed to be upbeat for both herself and Justin.

She surveyed the room. Glitter and paint littered the tables. Juice boxes overflowed the trashcan. As much as she wanted to go home, that couldn't happen until the mess left behind by tiny tornadoes was cleaned.

"Looks like a hurricane swept through here." Colt's voice over her shoulder jolted her with a thrill Danielle really shouldn't feel.

Swallowing the lump in her throat, she forced a smile, determined to hold on to the first friendly words he'd spoken in hours. "I was thinking the same thing." Tugging her ponytail tighter, she headed for the grouping of tables without looking his way. "If you want to help, there's a broom in the kitchen that—"

"I'm sorry."

His words caught her somewhere in the chest. Danielle stopped, eyes on the door leading to the kitchen. She didn't turn. "Why?"

"I couldn't talk Justin into staying."

The pain in the frank admission spoke of more than obligation. Something deeper lurked in the words, something that turned her toward him.

He was watching her, trying to gauge her reaction.

"Colt." Danielle took two steps toward him and stopped. "I couldn't stop him, either." And oh, how many times she'd tried. "It's not your fault."

"If there was some way I could have—"

A loud clatter from the kitchen whirled Colt toward the sound, hand at the pistol on his hip.

Danielle jumped and clutched her chest with a small shriek. Forcing her breath to slow, she identified the sound before Colt could cross the room to investigate. "Icemaker."

"You're sure?" He still eyed the door, his stance ready to take on whatever might plow through it.

"Yes. It's an industrial icemaker someone donated. Comes in really handy in the summer." With her hand over her heart, Danielle chuckled at her own jumpiness, working hard to ignore the fact that Colt was prepared to use the weapon at his side to protect her. "We couldn't hear it earlier because the kids sort of overpowered the sound." She snatched a trash bag, headed up the center of the tables arranged into a *U*, and swept an assortment of broken popsicle sticks and snack wrappers into the garbage. Gold glitter from a last-minute angel wings project stuck to her sweater and coated her hand. She'd be washing that off for days.

If she kept moving, she wouldn't have to face the push and pull of Colt's presence. "Like I said, there's a broom in the kitchen if you want to help." She stopped her work to watch his response. Maybe she'd finally get a smile.

"Is that a hint?" He chuckled as he locked the big double front door, his eyes darkening with concern when he shook it once and it wiggled more than it probably should. He eyed it for a second then turned and strode across the room toward the kitchen. "I'll help you in a few minutes so we can get you home for some rest." His gaze lingered on hers before he turned toward the kitchen. "When the kids left, our outside detail took off. I'm going to make one more circuit around the building."

"You worried about something outside?"

"Something feels weird and I can't put my finger on what it is. Maybe it's that icemaker of yours rattling back there." He gave her another forced smile then slipped through the swinging door into the kitchen.

That smile was definitely different than the one he'd given Kylie earlier.

Slapping her palm on the table and creating a gold glitter dust cloud, Danielle groaned. *Seriously. Get over it, girl. He might be the quarterback, but you're definitely not the head cheerleader.*

Clearly, she needed to stop watching teen movies

from the eighties in the dead of night while she waited up for Justin.

Grinning at her own idiocy, she turned to make her way up the other side of the tables.

Another crash and a thud from the kitchen clinched her fist around a balled up piece of paper. That wasn't the icemaker.

A door slammed and Danielle let the garbage bag drop to the floor with a soft clatter. "Colt?" When there was no answer, she spun toward the kitchen, her pulse beating in her head.

A wiry man stood at the end of the table, leering at her. His bleached blond hair spiked in every direction. A goatee shadowed his chin. His bare arms beneath his T-shirt sported multiple grim tattoos.

Danielle gasped. Her heart pounded in her ears as cold sweat broke out along her skin. Where was Colt?

She had to find him. To get out of here. To make it to the front door where people drove by on the street. Colt needed help. She needed safety.

The man took a step toward her, a triumphant grin twisting the corner of his mouth.

Danielle's feet froze to the floor. Her hand went instinctively to her hip pocket, where her phone usually was.

Empty. Her eyes darted the room. It was on the table right next to the man who was slowly stepping toward her, seeming to take pleasure in her fear.

Following her gaze, his landed on the phone, as well. With a snake-like whip of his wrist, he swept the device to the floor, then crunched it beneath the heel of his boot.

Danielle jumped, a scream lodging in her throat.

Colt! She scrambled backward, tripping over the table behind her. Losing her balance, she caught herself and darted toward the opening she'd created, eyes on the kitchen door. Safety was only ten feet away.

A force caught her hair and jerked her backward, dragging a cry from her throat. Her hair pulled tighter against her scalp as the man wound it around his hands, dragging her toward him, pulling her head back next to his.

His hot breath brushed her ear as he growled, "Don't you dare scream, love." The British accent raked across her skin, unexpected and menacing.

Danielle whimpered as he dragged her closer, snaking an arm around her waist and lifting her off her feet. Colt was in as much danger as she was. The thought swam in her stomach, which was threatening to revolt.

His whisper was harsh against the skin of her neck. "Should have sent a stronger man to protect a pretty lady like you."

Danielle struggled and fought, but his arm was too tight around her. He had her pinned, her head pulled back at an awkward angle by her hair. Her eyes stung and watered.

He carried her between the tables, muttering as she fought, words that would have made her mother ground her for years if Danielle had dared to utter them out loud.

If he reached the back door with her, she was done.

Tears stung her eyes. Her brother. He'd never forgive himself for leaving her.

And Colt...

Danielle fought harder, trying to throw an elbow at her kidnapper. He stopped in the center of the room and jerked her hair harder, pulling at her neck. "Do it again and I use the knife I brought. Rio Garcia wants you alive but eh, accidents happen."

Danielle froze. This was no game.

And her life was of no consequence to this man.

ELEVEN

Something in the back of Colt's mind screamed danger. He'd made a sweep of the back parking lot and checked an empty car parked on the street close to the Mission, but nothing seemed out of place. Still, he couldn't shake the innate feeling that the whole thing was about to blow up on him.

He ought to make a full circuit of the building, but the alarm bells screaming in his head said leaving the unlocked kitchen door unguarded was asking for trouble. Leaving Danielle unprotected inside for more than a moment felt like the height of foolishness as it was.

Stopping with his hand on the handle of the kitchen door, he let his eyes sweep the brick of the building. Maybe nothing was wrong out here. Maybe there wasn't any additional danger lurking in the shadows.

Maybe he was simply all stirred up because everything between him and Danielle had skidded sideways with that moment that passed between them last night. She'd been standoffish with him all day, the warm ease between them chilling into ice. If anything was wrong in the world, that was it.

Maybe he really should tell Vance he needed to be off this detail.

Resolving to do just that before either he or Danielle was hurt, Colt lifted his head to go into the kitchen.

Motion in the reflection of the glass caught his eye, and he kept a practiced stillness. Behind him, the shadow of a man stepped closer, nearing the bottom of the stairs.

Pulling in a deep breath, Colt drew his pistol at the same time he whipped around on the small stoop, keeping the weapon leveled on the man who stood just two steps beneath him.

Eyes widening in quick surprise, the guy took one step back, just out of Colt's reach. He was tall and heavyset, his arms covered in the same types of tattoos he'd seen on the young men who'd left with Justin, but this guy was older, harder. His demeanor was less cocky, more violently confident. In his hand, he gripped a thick knife.

Heart pounding harder, Colt stared at the man without wavering. His gut had been right. Something was about to go down. "Drop it. Now."

Dark eyes narrowed, the black gaze of his would-be attacker never leaving his.

Colt had been in enough standoffs to know the guy was weighing his options, and he was just as likely to lunge as he was to run. Letting his finger slip to the trigger, Colt steeled himself for whatever came.

The motion must have been obvious. After two rapid blinks, the man launched off the steps in a dead run for the street.

On a burst of adrenaline, Colt followed to the corner, his boots pounding on the pavement, but he skidded to a halt at the street. He couldn't leave Danielle. Had to get back inside to her right now. This could be the beginning of a much bigger strike. Ripping his cell phone from his pocket, Colt pressed the emergency number for dispatch as he ran back across the parking lot. "I need backup now. We've got trouble at the Mission." He gave a quick description of the runner and the direction he'd fled, then cut the call and reached for the back door, jerking it hard.

Nothing.

Fear and dread blended in his veins. Knowing he wouldn't be out of sight of the door, he'd left it unlocked.

Something was definitely wrong.

There was no way he'd be able to breach the heavy metal door with its thick glass window, but the rickety front double doors… That would have to be the way in.

He charged around the building, gun drawn, praying the sounds of approaching sirens were heading his way. There wasn't much time. If the man he'd run off had been sent to do away with him, it was possible there were others in play coming after Danielle.

Rounding the corner, he glanced around the parking lot, took in the light traffic on the street, swept his gaze across Danielle's little two-door car, then raced up the steps to the double doors, already gauging how much force it would take to get into the building.

A muffled crash echoed against the door. A man cried out.

"Colt!" Danielle screamed, his name muffled at the end.

Adrenaline smacked Colt in the chest, punching his heart into overdrive.

Hopefully, Danielle's friend Zoe would forgive

him…and hopefully whoever was inside with Danielle was unarmed.

Colt braced one foot on the ground and kicked his heel hard at the seam between the two front doors, just above the lock.

The wood splintered as the door burst inward. Colt raised his weapon with both hands and went in sighting the space.

About fifteen feet away, at the end of the U-shaped table arrangement, a tall blond man had Danielle by the hair and around the waist. His thin forearm bore multiple tattoos.

Peter Sullivan. Looked like "Limey Pete" had graduated from harboring fugitives to kidnapping. He'd obviously been in the act of hauling Danielle toward the back of the building, where he'd probably assumed his partner had done away with Colt. Now he stood in the kitchen doorway, staring at Colt in mild shock.

Colt caught a slim sight line on Sullivan but not enough to pull the trigger without risking Danielle, who stared at him, her dark eyes wide and frantic.

His heart hammered against his ribs. All he wanted was to dive straight at the man and rip Danielle from his arms.

That went against everything he'd been trained to do. Pulling in a deep breath, Colt held the weapon steady, centering himself in the moment, in grabbing the bad guy and saving his target.

He couldn't think of her as Danielle, as the woman who had definitely gotten under his skin. It would strip him of his tactical advantage, allow his emotions to control the show. He stepped sideways around the tables, edging around to the right, trying to get a clear line on the man who held Danielle tightly and was edging for the kitchen door again. "Let her go, Sullivan." The command in his voice left no room for argument, no question as to how this would end if Peter Sullivan didn't obey.

Pete chuckled. "Let her go?" He turned his head and nuzzled Danielle's hair as she cringed, her face tightening in abject terror. "The bird smells so nice. I'm sure you understand."

Colt understood his blood was boiling beneath the surface of his skin. He understood he was a heartbeat away from striding across the room and tearing the punk's arm off. But he couldn't let any of that show in his stance or on his face. It would throw the advantage to his adversary and Danielle would be gone.

There had to be a way to get her out of Sullivan's hands.

"How much for the woman? What's Garcia paying?" As he spoke, Colt edged around another step, toward a chair that was pulled out from the table closest to him. Keep the guy talking and he'd stop focusing on what Colt was doing as he maneuvered into position.

. Sullivan backed away a step. "More than you have in your pocket, mate."

Holstering his weapon, Colt held up both hands. If this went sideways, his weapon was useless anyway. He'd have to trust his strength against a man who was probably skilled in no-holds-barred street fighting.

His pulse thundered in his ears. If this didn't work, he could get Danielle killed or, worse, taken away forever and sold into who knew what when Garcia figured out she wasn't his sister. The thought chilled his insides into ice. "Tell you what. I look the other way, you give me ten percent. You take her. No fight." He shot Danielle a hard look, dropping his eyes to the floor and back up to hers again.

The fear in her expression eased, and she blinked twice.

"We have a deal? You get the girl, I get my cut? Otherwise, you and I both know this isn't going to end well for either of us."

Peter Sullivan hesitated, his grip on Danielle loosening, as though he couldn't hold her and think at the same time.

On cue, Danielle jerked her head forward, loosening her hair from his grip, and dropped to the floor.

Colt jumped, one step onto the chair, one onto the table, and made a flying leap onto Sullivan, his shoulder driving into the other man's chest. They crashed to the floor, Colt with the advantage as the other man's head cracked against the tile floor and he lay still.

Rolling Sullivan onto his stomach, Colt cuffed him, then sat back on his heels and dropped his chin to his chest, hauling in deep breaths before he stood. Jerking his phone from his pocket, he made a terse call to dispatch before turning to Danielle, who'd backed against one of the tables. He held out his arm to her. "Come here."

She was beside him in an instant, her head buried in his shoulder, her hands between them at his chest. She trembled with silent sobs as Colt slipped his arms around her and pulled her to him, relief weakening him until he was pretty sure he was going to start shaking right along with her. Here he was again, a failure. As soon as Major Vance found out, he might be pulled off this mission, too. Too unreliable to go after Garcia, too undependable to protect Danielle… He was clearly the weak link.

Everybody knew it.

Although Danielle was safe for now, the call had been too close for anybody's liking. She never should have had to suffer through this or the nightmares that were likely to follow.

Colt brushed a kiss against her hair. For one more second, he'd let himself have this, Danielle secure in his arms where nothing could harm her.

Just one more second…

TWELVE

"What's for dinner?"

Danielle jumped when Justin spoke behind her, dropping the pot she'd been filling at the sink. A wave of water sloshed along the inside of the sink and rolled back, crashing to the floor at her feet. She jumped away, hand to her chest as water seeped through her socks and soaked her toes. "What is wrong with you, Justin? You scared me to death!"

Her brother backed into the living room, his hands in the air in a gesture of surrender. "Whoa. It's only dinner, okay? Whatever you cook is fine."

Snatching the dishrag from the handle of the stove, Danielle leaned over and swiped at the water on the floor. She shouldn't have snapped at her brother but, right now, it felt like kidnappers and armed men lurked in every corner. It wasn't so farfetched to imagine they'd wandered into her own kitchen. "It's okay. I'm just jumpy."

"Something else happened?" Justin didn't come closer, but his dark head tilted in question.

"Does something else have to happen for me to be on edge?" Danielle sat back on her heels and swiped her hair out of her face with her wrist. After they'd wrapped up at the Mission, she'd told Colt not to let Justin know there'd been another incident. It might push him in even deeper with this group he couldn't seem to stay away from, convince him all the more that he needed a gun to protect their family. She dipped her head and swiped at the giant spill again, hating the fact she had to keep the truth from her own brother.

Another presence knelt beside her and a warm hand rested on hers.

Colt.

Lifting her hand, he gently pulled the towel from her fingers and leaned closer to whisper in her ear. "Let me handle this."

Man, how she wanted him to. His touch blew all the way through her, warming her heart in ways no man ever had. Colt had proven how capable he was of handling whatever the Garcia cartel threw at them. Of sharing the heavy load she'd carried alone for far too long.

He was only a couple of inches away, his strong chest inviting, especially when she could still feel the power of it beneath her hands as he'd held her at the Mission. For the first time in days, maybe even years, she'd felt perfectly, entirely safe.

Perfectly, entirely treasured.

No. He belonged to somebody else. Danielle rocketed to her feet and edged away from him, her hip colliding with the counter. "I'm fine. I need to cook. I have to keep moving or..." She glanced at Justin, who still watched from the living room. "It just helps me to keep going."

From where he rested on one knee on the floor, Colt

looked up at her as though his brown eyes could see right into her soul.

Oh, to sink into that look and stay there.

She turned away, snatched up the pot and started filling it again. It was a long moment before Colt went back to drying the floor then stood behind her, so close she could feel his hesitation. Finally, he crossed to the refrigerator and leaned against it to watch her. Even though he was on what amounted to the other side of the kitchen, the room was so small he was still only a few feet away.

When she turned to put the pot on the stove, Justin leaned on his forearms on the small counter that separated the kitchen from the living room, his gaze bouncing back and forth between Colt and Danielle. When he caught her watching him, he stopped. "So you never told me what we're eating."

"Lasagna." Making the dish involved enough steps to keep her mind occupied, but the recipe was easy enough to leave room for any inevitable mistakes. She had to keep moving or she'd sink to the floor and curl into a ball, either from fear or from grief. Colt, Kylie and another Ranger—Austin, maybe?—had convinced her she needed to stay away from the Mission for the time being. It hadn't been a hard sell. She'd spent the past few hours wondering what would have happened if that horrible man had arrived five minutes earlier when all of the children were still there. She was a danger to all of them if she stayed, but it was breaking her heart to keep her distance, especially with the Christmas party only a couple of days away.

When she looked up, both men had laser gazes right on her.

Seriously? She needed her space. "Food will be ready in an hour. Staring at me won't make this go any faster."

Justin grinned and shoved off from the counter, but he didn't walk away. Instead he looked at Colt. "So, that other lady, the Border Patrol Agent... Is she coming by?" He glanced at his watch. "Shouldn't she be here by now?"

"I'm all you're getting tonight, buddy. Sorry. Kylie had to be somewhere else." Colt was biting back a grin. "And anyway, she's spoken for."

Danielle's stomach fell to her feet, dragging what was left of her appetite with it. There it was. Out in the open. The truth about Colt and Kylie. No pretending anymore.

Suddenly, lasagna seemed like a very bad idea. Just the smell of the garlic in her homemade sauce was enough to do her in.

"She's engaged." Colt nudged Danielle's foot with his. "You met the guy today. Austin."

Danielle's hand froze in the middle of mixing the cheeses. The words took a minute to compute. She had to dig for her voice, which had tucked tail and lodged itself in the middle of her throat. "Tall guy? Looks like an all-American superhero type?"

Colt snorted. "Tell me you didn't." He shook his head, muttering. "Superhero."

"He must be the guy who came to pick her up the other day." Justin chimed in from the short hallway on his way to the bedroom. He shut the door behind him, clearly finished with this conversation and more than a little dejected that Kylie wasn't coming...and that there was no hope.

Danielle could relate.

But wait. If Colt hadn't backed off because he was in a relationship with Kylie, then why had he pulled away from her? Was there someone else? Last night, he'd acted as though he were going to kiss her, then he'd shut down and been formal and work-oriented all day.

Then again, he'd held her close at the Mission after he'd rescued her, almost as though he was as desperate as she was. "Why?"

"Why what?"

She hadn't realized the word had come out. Fiddling with the bowl on the counter, she bit the inside of her lower lip, glanced at the floor, the cabinet, the ceiling… anything but Colt.

"Why what, Danielle?" His voice was low, intimate, too close in the small space.

Mouth suddenly dry, she swallowed a couple of times and splayed her hands on the counter. "Why did you hold me the way you did today?"

Silence.

When she looked up, Colt hadn't moved. It was as though time had stopped. He simply stood, leaning against the refrigerator, his arms crossed over his chest, pulling his dark gray shirt tight across his shoulders. He was watching her, something in his eyes drawing her closer, making her want to cross the room to stand in his arms again. The air between them zipped with electricity that struck her in the chest and flushed her skin. Powerless to stop herself, she turned fully toward him, almost without realizing she'd moved.

Colt straightened. His eyes never left hers as his expression shifted to something Danielle couldn't interpret. His gaze dipped to her lips and came back to her eyes with a silent question that demanded an answer.

He must have seen her thoughts, because he was across the room in two strides, his palms on her cheeks, his fingers in her hair…his lips on hers.

Everything vanished but him. Desperate to have him closer, she grabbed fistfuls of his shirt, losing herself to him, falling into something she'd never dared to dream about, never dared to ask for, but never wanted to lose.

His fingers trailed down her neck as he eased into the kiss. He pressed his forehead to hers, breathing heavily, then brushed a kiss across her cheek and found her lips again, folding her into his arms.

It was both the safest and most dangerous place she'd ever been.

A rustle from the hallway shattered the dream, and Danielle jumped backward, her hip colliding with the handle on the stove, her hands shaking and ears ringing.

Colt stood where she'd left him, looking as stunned as she felt.

Eyes on his phone, Justin walked into the living room. "I'm out. See you guys later."

Tearing her gaze from Colt's, Danielle fought to center herself in a reality much colder than the fantasy she'd been drifting in. She blinked a couple of times as Justin headed for the door, shrugging into his coat. "Where are you going?"

Shoving his hands into his jacket pockets, he whirled on Danielle, his squared shoulders holding a defiant challenge. "Out."

Danielle flicked a quick glance at Colt, who was watching with concern, his eyebrows pulled into a deep V as he straightened and followed her silently into the living room. "I thought you were staying for dinner."

"I got a phone call. The guys are hanging out tonight

and I'm going. More fun than watching you two make eyes at each other, ya know?"

From over her shoulder, Colt cleared his throat. "Justin, I don't think—"

"I told you the other night. My sister's your business. I'm not." Jerking his hands from his pockets, Justin grabbed the doorknob and yanked the door open, a cold breeze blasting into the apartment and blowing a piece of paper that had fallen from his pocket across the room toward the Christmas tree. "I'm out. Don't wait up for me." Without looking back, he shut the door with a little more force than necessary.

Danielle sagged against the counter and pressed her palms against her eyes, willing herself not to cry. Five minutes ago, her brother had seemed like his old self, laughing and asking about Kylie. Two minutes ago, she'd held the world in her hands. Now, everything shattered at her feet in shards of icy reality.

Colt laid his hand on her back, between her shoulder blades. "Danielle..."

She shrugged him off. Her focus should have been on her brother, not on the man beside her, no matter how her heart pulled her to him. She had to get away, to clear her head and to guard her heart.

The scent of tomatoes, cheese and garlic hung too powerfully in the air, twisting her stomach and almost making her gag. Unable to speak and release the pressure, she strode to her bedroom, shut the door and sank against it, burying her face in her hands, wishing the tears would come instead of jamming up in a throbbing knot in her throat. Justin could be doing all sorts of things in the dark hours he stayed away from home. Every day, his demeanor changed a little bit more, and he stayed away a little later. One day, he might not come back to her at all. *Dear Lord, help me. Help my brother.*

Her brother. Was he still her kid brother, or had he somehow wandered to a dark side he'd never be able to escape?

Leaning heavily against the counter that separated the kitchen from the rest of the apartment, Colt dragged a hand down his face and tipped his head toward the ceiling. His heartbeat still pounded in his chest, and his skin still felt flushed from kissing Danielle. What was he thinking?

His chest was still warm from the touch of her hands. He could still feel the way she'd molded against him. For one small moment, his heart of stone had melted into one of flesh. He'd felt alive. Warm.

What had he done? He should have been the hard case, the one who'd never let a woman fell him.

From Danielle's bedroom door just a few feet away, he could hear her muttering in Spanish. A few words came clearly through the jumble. Jesus. Help. *Mi hermano...* My brother.

The same cries his heart had pleaded silently so many times when he was younger. The ones he'd screamed out loud as Caleb bled out in his arms.

There hadn't been an answer then. Would there be one now? Maybe Danielle's faith was stronger than his. Maybe she understood something he didn't. Maybe God was more willing to listen to someone like her.

Feeling helpless, wanting to go to her yet knowing she needed her space, Colt wandered into the kitchen, clicked off the stove, and stared at the food scattered across the counter. He'd never had lasagna outside of a restaurant. If he had any know-how at all, he'd finish the dish and leave it for Danielle. She needed her strength. But since his forte was microwave dinners…

Colt gathered the food, then shoved it into the fridge and put the dishes in the dishwasher, desperate to do something tangible for the woman whose prayers still filtered in low murmurs through the door, bringing a crushing pain to his chest.

Lord, if You're listening, comfort Danielle and save her brother.

Slamming the dishwasher shut, he pressed the start button then wandered into the den. His job here was to pull surveillance and protect Danielle Segovia, so he might as well do it, no matter how much he wanted to break down her door and kiss her again.

He definitely couldn't do that. Pulling back the curtain, Colt surveyed the parking lot. Nothing moved in the shadows.

It sure would be nice to have backup out there, but everyone was tied up on the mission to catch Garcia's shipment coming across the border. Here he sat on the night before Christmas Eve, staring at a dark parking lot with a dark Christmas tree behind him, a broken, terrified woman appealing to God only a few feet away… and a young man so like his brother walking the same inevitable deadly path.

Colt dropped the curtain into place. He was a failure on all counts. He might as well turn in his badge and take a job as a security guard somewhere. He'd do a lot less damage.

But that would mean he'd have to turn his back on Danielle. Even if he was helpless to make this all better, he couldn't abandon her, not after he'd kissed her.

Not after he'd finally let himself acknowledge he might possibly be falling in love with her.

He flicked a wooden snowflake ornament on the Christmas tree and balled his fists, willing himself not to go knock on her door, pull her to him and tell her he would shield her from the world. That would definitely push the boundaries of his job.

Not that he hadn't shattered those boundaries already. When he'd mentioned Kylie's engagement to Austin, something had changed in Danielle's demeanor. She'd looked at him with eyes that invited him closer. He'd been helpless to keep from going to her.

It was either the smartest thing he'd ever done or the absolute dumbest.

"Colt." Her voice came from behind him, a low whisper.

Steeling himself against the sight of her, he turned, shoving his hands into his pockets to keep from reaching out. Her eyes were red, her face flushed. She looked forlorn and lost standing just a few feet away.

God, help me. He couldn't shut her out now.

He held out his arms and she stepped into them, burying her face in his neck. "What am I supposed to do?"

Pressing a kiss to the top of her head, he pulled away, tucking a lock of her deep brown hair behind her ear. "You keep praying. Keep loving him."

She nodded and pulled away, drifting toward the Christmas tree.

They needed to talk about what had happened between them, but now wasn't the time. Right now, she was focused on being Justin's sister, scared for her brother, scared for herself... She didn't need the man who was supposed to be protecting her adding to the weight she carried.

Danielle plugged in the tree, then snagged a piece of paper from the floor, unfolding it as she spoke. "I'm going to finish dinner. I'm not hungry, but I need to..." Her forehead wrinkled as she stared at the paper in her hand.

"What is it?"

She passed it to Colt, then headed for the kitchen. "Who knows? I think Justin dropped it, but it looks like he was doodling in class or something."

Glancing at the small quarter sheet of paper, Colt felt his blood chill. A flowing river sketched in pencil filled the space. A large canvas-style bag was drawn on one side, and a rope snaked across the other.

He knew those symbols, had studied them intently since the Garcia cartel had moved to the center of the Rangers' radar. The bag indicated movement of a shipment. The river showed the mode of transportation. The rope... That was a new one.

It didn't matter. The cartel operated by sending messages up and down the chain in cryptic drawings like this one. With his team on the way to a drug drop across the river, this had to be a message about that exact mission. The only way Justin Segovia had possession of a message from the cartel was if he was a part of the transfer.

Justin was in bigger danger than even Danielle's worst nightmares had ever dreamed, in worse danger than even Caleb had been in...

And Colt had let his little brother die on his watch.

Not Justin. He would not lose Justin Segovia, would not let Danielle suffer the pain he'd carried for a decade.

"Colt?"

He glanced at her, then shoved the paper in his pocket.

She was undeterred. "You know where Justin is. You know what he's doing, don't you? There's something on that paper that told you—some kind of coded message."

Colt stood there, clenching and unclenching his fists. He had to do something to stop Justin. This was his chance to prove to himself and to his team that he still had the gut instinct to do his job.

But he had to protect Danielle. He couldn't leave her alone. Not now. Not when it was clear Garcia was still determined to take her.

Danielle stood in the center of the kitchen, holding the bowl Colt had shoved into the refrigerator just moments before, looking at him with determination in her eyes. Setting the bowl down, she rounded the counter and stood toe to toe with him. "You have to go find my brother."

She had no idea how badly he wanted to, but he couldn't just walk out on her. It was too dangerous. "I'm not leaving you here alone. I'll call backup to come in." With the bulk of the team on the mission to catch Garcia, help would be slow to come, though. Still…

"It will take too long." It was as though she read his mind. "You have to find him. I'll be okay. Please." Her voice broke on the *please*, shattering the last of Colt's common sense. He couldn't deny her the very thing his own heart wanted.

Here he was, caught between duty to his job and his growing obligations to a woman whose heart's cry mirrored his own. "Fine, but you have to do what I say." Colt held his hands out to the side and backed away from her, holding her gaze, trying to communicate how serious his next command would be. "I know your cell is gone, but call me on the house phone if you need me. Lock the door. Double lock it. Put a chair in front of it if you have to. Whatever you do, don't open the door for anybody except me. Not even Justin."

"But he's—"

The crack in her voice tore at him, but he had no reassurances for her. "Promise me, or I stay right here and we wait for backup."

"If he comes back, I—"

"You call me and keep the door locked. Now promise."

She stepped backward at the authority in his voice, her eyes wide. Finally, she nodded once.

Colt pulled open the door and stepped into the night, taking the stairs down two at a time. As he dialed dispatch's number for backup, he knew this was foolish, yet he prayed for his mission to be successful and for both of the Segovias to be safe.

THIRTEEN

Shoving the entire lasagna into the refrigerator, Danielle shut the door and leaned her forehead against the cool white exterior, staring at the floor beneath her feet. It practically gleamed. She'd finished preparing the lasagna, put it in the oven, wandered the apartment for half an hour, then attacked the floor with a bucket of soapy water and a brush. She had to keep moving or she'd find herself staring at the wall, imagining the worst.

It had been nearly an hour since Justin and Colt had left. Justin wasn't answering his phone. Colt had called before he was even out of the parking lot to tell her an El Paso police officer was on the way to stand guard outside. She didn't dare reach out to him again or he might think she was in trouble and break off the search for her brother. Whatever had been on that piece of paper, it had been enough to drive Colt out of here on a mission.

A mission that included not letting her brother into their own apartment.

That wasn't something she could handle thinking about.

Wrapping her arms around her middle, Danielle

turned and leaned against the fridge, imagining she could still feel the warmth from Colt standing in the exact same spot earlier.

Embarrassment heated her cheeks. This was exactly like middle school, when she'd tucked her red knit glove under her pillow for months, the one she'd been wearing when Noah Wilson held her hand during a football game.

Surely she was beyond childish stuff like that.

Even if Colt tried to dodge her when he got back, they had some talking to do. Soon. Neither one of them could go on any longer in this twisted dance.

The talking would extend to her brother, as well. No longer would Justin get to walk all over her the way he'd done lately. Sure, he was older now, feeling his own way in the world, but she was his guardian for a few more years and he had to listen to her. It was time to take her authority back and remind him of that. Whether he liked it or not, he was about to start keeping a curfew and stop hanging around with guys that were definitely nothing but trouble.

With a nod to her own agreement, Danielle flipped the kitchen light switch and drifted into the small living room. There was nothing to do now but wait.

Or she could clean the bathroom.

The key turned in the lock, and the door opened, catching on the chain with a dull thud.

Danielle shrieked, slapping her hand over her mouth as her heart jumped into her throat.

"Dani?" Justin's voice came through the crack, thin and plaintive. "Why's the chain on the door?"

Whatever you do, don't open the door for anybody except me. Not even Justin.

"Dani?" His voice grew louder and he rattled the door against the chain. "Can you hear me?"

Pressing her fingertips against her lips so hard her teeth bit into the tender flesh, she stared at the door. This was her brother. She'd practically raised him.

But Colt said…

Colt. Who'd been back and forth with her all day. Who'd kissed her and run. Who'd only shown up in her life a few days ago.

Versus her brother.

This was like a bad horror movie. Her brother was on the other side of the door, not some body-snatched alien impersonator. The events of the past few days had her head twisted around. If she couldn't trust Justin, she might as well change her identity and move to another state.

Swallowing what was left of her fear, Danielle strode for the door. "Coming."

She shut the door, unlatched the chain, then pulled it open again. "Sorry. I'm just paranoid."

Justin stood in the hallway, staring at her with wide, dark eyes. He didn't cross the threshold, just shoved his hands in his pockets, glanced up the hallway, then looked back at her. "Is Colt here?"

Alarm bells rang in her head, loud and clanging. Justin's expression was tight, the lines around his mouth more about fear than anger. Danielle reached for his elbow to drag him into the apartment. "He left right after you did. Get in—"

Justin stumbled toward Danielle as though he'd been shoved, colliding with her and staggering them both backward. Her back caught on the edge of the bar that divided the kitchen from the rest of the apartment, the pain sharp enough to draw a gasp.

The door slammed and Justin stumbled to the side.

A man she'd never seen before stood in the living room. His dark eyes glittered. He was shorter than her and stocky. His mouth twisted in a wry smile.

He held a pistol that he aimed at Justin, who stood in the center of the living room with his hands in the air. "Don't hurt my sister, William." His voice cracked with tension.

Danielle's pulse pounded in her temples. She couldn't take her eyes off the gun. She had to get between it and Justin. It was her job to protect her brother.

Skittering sideways, she stood in front of Justin, arms out to protect him behind her. "What do you want?" The forceful voice couldn't have come from her lips. Her insides were shuddering too hard.

"You."

"No." Justin tried to shove around Danielle, but she sidestepped to keep herself between the gun and her brother.

He couldn't put himself in the line of fire. Couldn't get hurt trying to protect her.

"Don't worry, J. I don't want to shoot Danielle here, if that's really her name." William kept his eyes sharp on Danielle. "But shooting you isn't a problem."

Danielle gasped, took a step back and collided with her brother. "Don't." Her throat was tight, her voice stretched thin. It didn't matter what happened to her. Justin had to stay safe. *Colt, where are you?* If she kept William talking, maybe he'd come back. "Tell me what you want."

"You to come with me."

"Where?"

Laughing, William shook his head, keeping the gun aimed slightly to the right of Danielle's head. "You don't get to ask. If you cooperate, you get to walk down the stairs where my friend will meet you. When you're safely in the car, I'll walk away and leave Justin here safe and sound. If you don't cooperate, Justin will get shot and you'll get dragged to the car anyway."

"Dani, don't." Justin's voice broke. His hands latched onto her shoulders. "Don't trust him."

"That hurts, man. I thought we were friends." A mocking pout on his face, William gestured to the side with the gun. "Let her go, J. She's not your sister. She's the sister of a more important man, and he wants her back."

That was what this was about. More people coming at her, trying to take her to a man who had no idea who she really was. "I'm not who you think I am."

"Nice try."

"She's telling the truth." Colt's voice came from the breezeway and he appeared in the doorway, pistol raised, barrel aimed at the back of William's head. He never looked at Danielle or Justin. "Put the gun down before I put it down for you." His voice was commanding, hard, leaving no room to doubt that he'd do exactly what he'd threatened if pushed.

Danielle's heart pounded harder, her knees almost giving out. She reached for the counter to hold herself up. He'd come back. He'd saved her. Again.

William's eyes widened as his jaw slackened, his mouth opening, then closing again. The gun he held wavered but remained fixed squarely on Justin.

"Put it down. Slowly." Colt stepped sideways around William toward Danielle, keeping his distance, his aim never faltering. "If you try anything, that door behind you is wide open and there's a trained sniper with his sights on you. You won't get far. We've got your friend downstairs in custody. It's over."

Visibly shaking, William opened his hand and let the pistol dangle from one finger, then knelt and settled in on the floor.

Without lowering his weapon, Colt held his stance as uniformed officers appeared, one taking possession of the pistol as another handcuffed William and led him away.

"I'll be down in a minute," Colt told the officer. Breathing heavily, he holstered his gun and turned to Danielle for the first time.

She wanted to throw herself into his arms, but her feet were frozen to the floor.

"Are you two okay?"

She nodded, then turned to her brother, who pulled her close. "Dani, I'm sorry. I'm so sorry. I had no idea. You kept trying to tell me. You kept saying... You were right. They're bad, those guys."

Danielle held her brother close, the way she used to when he was small, although he towered over her now. "It's okay. You're safe. It's okay." She desperately wanted it to be. But if Garcia was willing to come at her in full-on blast mode like this, he was likely to do anything.

She glanced over her shoulder, desperate for a glimpse of Colt.

But the door was closed, and he was gone.

Colt took the stairs to Danielle's apartment two at a time. It had been an hour since he'd left her and Justin in the capable hands of an El Paso police officer and a detective who was taking their statement. The whole time he'd been wrapping things up downstairs, coordinating with the local law enforcement officers on securing the scene and protecting Danielle, his mind had been half on the job and half on getting back upstairs.

He'd seen with his own eyes that Danielle and Justin were both safe, but it wasn't enough. He needed to look her in the eye, touch her...

Tell her he was sorry.

Two quick raps on the door, then he twisted the knob and walked in.

Danielle jumped up from the couch where she was sitting with Justin, her hand going to her chest. She took two steps toward him them stopped, uncertainty ghosting over her features.

Colt couldn't blame her. He'd lost his head and kissed her, had accepted everything she'd given him and then left her alone. Instead of using his head, he'd let his emotions con him into doing her bidding and running off after her brother rather than staying to protect her.

Then the worst had happened. He could rail at her for disobeying his command. In fact, he'd spent the better part of the past hour angry that she'd opened the door.

Then he'd come to his own conclusion... If it had been Caleb on the other side of the door, he'd have done the same thing.

It almost physically hurt to look at her, but he stopped halfway in the room and opened his arms.

She was in them in an instant, her hair soft against his cheek.

"I am so sorry." He whispered the words against her hair. They weren't enough but it would have to do for now. He could have lost her, and all because his heart had been running the show instead of his head. Because he'd kissed her, then he'd chased after her brother instead of sitting right where he should have been, in the apartment with Danielle. Sure, he'd left someone standing guard in his stead. Had called in to headquarters to alert them. He'd done everything by the book, but he still probably deserved to be stripped of the badge he'd only pinned on a couple of years before.

All of that could come later. Right now, he had to deal with other things. If Justin had been inside a group connected to the cartel, even for a moment, he might have intel they could use against Garcia. Sure, the police had already questioned him, but Colt's questions would be different.

He released Danielle and turned the focus to Justin. Trying to track the younger man, he'd gone back to Peter Sullivan's house, but there had been little activity there. Only one light had burned in a window, and only one car sat in the driveway. It was possible they'd cleared out now that "Limey Pete" was in custody.

Colt had been almost back to the apartment when Justin's frantic text came in. *They're coming for Dani. Can't reach her.*

The officer he'd requested to watch the apartment hadn't had time to arrive, so there was no one to check on Danielle. It felt like hours instead of minutes before he got back to the apartment, calling dispatch for backup as he flew through the streets of El Paso. Two patrol cars had met him there and they'd taken both men into custody.

Now he had to find a way to make this right.

Justin jumped to his feet. "Colt. I'm sorry. They set

up a decoy and got the cop's attention and snuck up here. I should have—"

"You did the right thing." With a quick glance at Danielle, he crossed the room, laid a hand on Justin's shoulder and sank to the couch beside him. What he really wanted to do was wrap Danielle in his arms again and apologize until the day he died.

But right now, Justin was the more pressing matter.

"I told him that." Danielle's voice was low, heavy with the fear and concern she'd been hammered with over the past few hours.

Justin shook his head. "I didn't know what they were really doing. All I did was run errands for them. Then one of them found out about Danielle, said she wasn't really my sister, she was somebody else. William heard it. He…"

"It's over now." Colt sat forward on the couch so he could look Justin in the eye. "You did the right thing texting me."

"Dani put your number in my phone. William shoved me in the backseat after telling me we were coming to get Danielle, but he didn't take my phone. If he had—"

"He didn't." Colt dropped his head to the back of the couch and stared at the ceiling. If only Caleb had done the right thing the night he died. If only he'd called somebody, anybody, to ask for help before it was too late.

Justin grabbed Colt by the wrist. Gone was the defiant youth who'd stalked out of the house earlier. In his place was a scared kid who realized the danger he'd been playing with. "You have to help me get out."

The words twisted Colt's stomach. If only Caleb had said the same thing. He sat straighter, then stood and paced to the TV and back again. "You'll have to tell me everything you know. Everything you've seen or heard, even if it didn't seem like that big of a deal to you."

"I already told the police—"

"I'm listening for things they aren't. They'll give me a report on what you said, but you're the one who can give me details. Did you hear any plans? Learn any names?"

Justin's shoulders drooped. "Until tonight, all we talked about was video games and movies. I made money running packages, but I never knew what was in them."

"Is that what the note you dropped on the floor tonight was about?"

With a slow nod, Justin kept his eyes on the floor. "I never saw a note like that before." He shook his head. "William told me to drop it where you'd see it. Said it might be fun to mess with you."

Colt's muscles tightened. The whole thing had been a coordinated trap and he'd walked right into it. He really ought to resign. He should have seen it coming. Should have... Should have done anything but followed Justin at Danielle's request.

But right now, he needed information, not self-recrimination. Justin was their best link to Garcia at the moment. "Where did you deliver packages?" Maybe it would lead them to another safe house.

"Between the diner and a house around the corner."

It was a start. He'd known about Peter Sullivan's house. The diner was new information. "You ever peek in the packages?"

"No." Justin cast a glance at his sister as his ears reddened with shame. "I didn't want to know. If I didn't know, it might not be so bad. I could pretend…" He practically melted into the floor, his eyes cast down. "I'm just trying to help. Bagging groceries at the market isn't going to net enough to make a difference."

"You're actually on the way out of trouble." Colt couldn't be silent any longer. Justin needed to know the full truth, right now, while he was wavering. He had to understand that this could all end so much worse for both of them if he didn't leave the cartel and their easy money behind him.

That meant opening up parts of his life he'd never spoken about to anyone before.

"I'm going to tell you something not a lot of people know, and I need you to listen." Scrubbing the top of his head with his hand, Colt sat straighter on the couch, avoiding eye contact with both of them. He couldn't handle seeing rejection in Justin's eyes or pity in Danielle's. "When I was a senior in high school, my brother…" He cleared his throat, scratched his chin, stared at the ceiling…

The words stuck hard in his throat, boulders in a dam he'd spent years constructing.

"Caleb. He was a year younger than me and a lot like you. Got into his head after my dad left that he had to do something to help our mom. He was recruited by a gang of drug dealers. He was in longer and went deeper than you did." Colt swallowed bile. He had to tell this story, both to Justin and Danielle. "He went from small-time deliveries to dealing. The money was better."

Danielle seemed to freeze, her hand no longer moving on Justin's back. "Colt…" She gasped his name, almost as though she knew what was coming.

Whether she did or not, he wasn't stopping now. "I

found out about it from a buddy of mine who saw a deal go down between Caleb and another kid at school, one everybody knew was a druggie but nobody could ever catch red-handed. I tried to warn him…" Colt's gut felt as though he'd swallow those rocks jamming up his throat. *Lord, why is this so hard to say? Help me. Justin needs to know there are consequences if he stays on this road.* He had to say it if he had a chance of ever being healed. "He took off that night to do another deal. I was around the corner, looking for him when I heard the shot."

The echo had cracked off the surrounding buildings in the small downtown area. Hardly anyone on the sidewalks had paused, so common was the sound.

But Colt's feet had started running of their own volition, his sinking stomach telling him his little brother was in danger.

He'd skidded around the corner. A blue sedan flew out of the parking lot, the squeal of tires and thrown gravel carved out in its wake.

Caleb had lain facedown on the pavement next to his car. Sliding to his knees beside his brother, tearing holes in his jeans and shredding the skin on his knees, Colt hadn't felt the pain. His heart had thrummed in his ears. He'd heard himself screaming, but even now he couldn't remember the words. When he'd rolled Caleb onto his back, the sight of the wound in his chest had been too much to bear. He'd cradled his brother's shaking body in his lap as Caleb tried to speak, but the words wouldn't come through lips growing increasingly blue. Hands smeared with his brother's blood, Colt had dialed 911, but by the time the call connected, Caleb was staring glassy-eyed at the sky, his body already growing cold.

"Colt."

Colt's head shook once, drawing him back into the warmth of Danielle's living room. She had left her brother's side and knelt in front of him. Taking one of his hands in hers, she warmed his skin.

He looked away. He could still feel the slick warmth of his brother's blood, could smell the peculiar, sickening mixture of acrid gunpowder and coppery blood. It still haunted him every time someone was shot on the job—that smell, that sight, that sound... It had taken him well into army basic training to stop associating the crack of gunfire with instant death. After that, he'd become the best marksman in his unit, because the only way to beat the pain was to beat the bull's-eye. "Caleb bled out in my arms."

He finally hazarded a look into Danielle's eyes.

Tears wavered, deepening her brown eyes. She squeezed his hand. "It's over."

"It's never over." Not as long as the cartels preyed on the innocent and lured them in.

Slipping his hand from Danielle's, Colt stood and stepped around her, walking to the kitchen to stare into the sink. He'd nearly broken down in front of her and Justin. It was a weakness he never showed.

Yet it didn't feel like the brokenness he'd been expecting.

It felt like acceptance.

Healing.

FOURTEEN

The abject pain in Colt's expression swiped away the last of Danielle's own fear. She could break down later, when she was alone. Right now, Justin needed her to be the strong one, and Colt needed her to understand.

She stood by the couch and watched him in the kitchen as Justin sat silently staring at Colt's back.

"It's never over." Colt repeated the words and came back to stand beside her, staring down at Justin. "Never forget this. There are always more bad guys. Always more kids they'll exploit to do their dirty work. They sucked you in the same way they did Caleb, and if you stay with them then the ending will be the same." He shook his head, then lifted his chin, the uncertainty and pain slipping away as he took back the authority his badge afforded him. "This stops tonight. Do you understand?"

Danielle gasped. The way Justin had bucked against Colt's authority earlier, ordering him around might only make him rebel harder.

Justin stood, a new desperation in his expression. "They won't let me go easy. They've already said— "

"You've got me and your sister. And I'm a package

deal with a whole team of Texas Rangers. We'll handle this, but you have to do what we say. Understand?"

Justin nodded once, a level of misery on his face that Danielle hadn't witnessed since their parents were killed.

Danielle watched Colt, taking in the concern for her brother in his expression. The way he fought for her, for Justin, for the missing agent she'd overheard him mention to Kylie...

She probably shouldn't do it, but she reached for his hand. "I understand, too."

His fingers stayed stiff long enough for her to heat with shame at her actions, but then they twined with hers and he squeezed.

It was her turn to sag with relief. He'd accepted the gesture and her understanding. It all made sense now, the way he pulled away whenever she got close. The way he let the job drive him. The pain that lurked behind the determination in his gaze. He'd lost so much.

He was terrified of losing more. That had to be the reason he grew close then pulled back every single time.

Because the ugly, horrifying truth was that he could lose her, too, if Rio Garcia ever succeeded in taking her. And she could lose him if he was caught in the crossfire.

Right now, no matter what was simmering between the two of them, there were more immediate concerns.

Shuddering, she pulled her hand from his and stood ramrod straight beside him. She'd keep her distance, protect his heart, even if it meant ignoring hers.

"What now?" Justin looked up, still clearly miserable. "I led them here. They know where we live."

"They've always known where you lived."

The way Colt said them, the words crawled up Danielle's spine with a sense of ominous forboding. "What are you not telling me?" she asked.

Eyes widening briefly in a way that said he'd been caught, Colt froze, then reset his expression. "They hit you at work, Danielle. They've studied you."

"It's more than that." She turned toward him and pulled herself to her full height, even though that only brought her eyes to the level of his chin. She doubted he found her at all intimidating, but she was going to get answers from him all the same. This was her life. He didn't get to keep the details from her, even if they terrified her into yet another sleepless night. "Tell me."

He glanced at Justin then looked back at Danielle, opened his mouth, closed it. Finally, he exhaled loudly and crossed the room as though he were afraid she might take a swing at him. "Your car."

"What about my car?"

"The first night I was here, someone tried to sabotage it."

The air in her lungs huffed out in a rush, the room spinning slightly with the force of it. "The first night..." As realization dawned, fear drove a spike through her chest. "The day Kylie took my car in for an oil leak. There was no oil leak."

"Not a naturally occurring one." Colt gave a quick sketch of a man tampering with her car and of being attacked when he tried to pursue.

"That's why you were limping that day."

Colt nodded once.

"You could have told me."

"And had both of you even more frightened than you already were? No."

"Is there anything else—"

"No."

Scanning his face, Danielle looked for signs that he was holding more back. His expression was open, if a little tense.

He held out a hand to her, then dropped it to his side. "We have a police officer in the parking lot. I'll be bunking on your couch tonight. You're safe here." Colt turned to Justin. "You're on winter break from school, so there's no reason for you to leave this apartment. You go nowhere unless I'm with you or another Ranger that I've personally introduced you to escorts you."

Justin nodded, then tilted his head up with a gleam in his eye. "Can that other Ranger be Kylie?"

Danielle bit back a grin. If her brother was ready to make a joke, then he was going to be okay after all.

Coughing, Colt clearly tried to cover a laugh. "Agent Perry is with the Border Patrol. She was on loan to us and she's elsewhere now." He bit the inside of his lip and swallowed hard, probably trying not to embarrass Justin. "I'll pass along your hello to her, though."

Face pinking, Justin nodded. "Thanks."

"No problem." Colt jerked his chin toward the hallway. "If I were you, I'd grab a shower and some sleep." He flicked a glance at Danielle. "You, too. I know it won't be easy, but at least try."

As Justin walked out of the room, Danielle turned to Colt. "Tomorrow's Christmas Eve." The chaos of her life had buried any chance at holiday spirit, but she was bound and determined to celebrate her Savior's birth properly. He superseded everything else in her life, had gotten her through her parents' deaths... He'd get her through this. "I want to go to church."

"I know." His gaze swept her face, a mixture of regret and tenderness. "I also know that—" His phone buzzed, and he pulled it from his pocket and glanced at the screen. The line of his mouth tightened, and he didn't look up from the phone. "I have to go downstairs for a minute, but I'll be right back, and I'll be watching the door the whole time. As for tomorrow…we'll figure something out."

"Okay." It was a promise she'd hold him to.

With a lingering look that spoke more than words, he turned and pulled the door open, then disappeared into the cold night.

In a dark corner of the parking lot, Ranger Ethan Hilliard waited in a gray SUV. When he spotted Colt, he rolled down the window.

An in-person visit probably wasn't good news, not with almost all hands prepping for the op that Colt hoped would put a mighty big hurt on the man who was trying to take Danielle away from him.

Colt surveyed the parking lot as he strode across it, eyes attuned to anything out of place. With the direct hit on Danielle's home and the connection that the cartel had made to her brother, anything could happen at any time. After all, his own vehicle had already been a target.

Rio Garcia believed his sister had his money and his drugs, and he believed Danielle was his sister. The man was ruthless. Now that he knew for certain the Rangers were watching Danielle, he could escalate from trying to take her from under their noses to a full-blown frontal assault.

Looking for snipers, Colt scanned the trees at the edge of the parking lot. It wasn't exactly Garcia's style to employ military tactics, but at this point, anything could happen.

He was antsy and restless. Seeing that man with a gun aimed at Justin earlier had nearly stripped Colt of his professionalism. He'd wanted to pull the trigger, had nearly made a headlong dive at Danielle to knock her out of the way so he could take out the bad guy threatening her.

Totally against protocol.

Now that he'd told them what had happened to Caleb...

He shoved his hands into his pockets. They were still shaking. He'd been fighting for the past two hours to clear the images from his mind, to stop himself from mentally transposing Justin's face onto his brother's body. It could have gone down that way tonight, Justin bleeding to death because Colt had left his post.

"What's with the face?" Hilliard turned down the radio and hooked an elbow out the open window.

"Long day. Too much excitement." True enough, even if it wasn't the whole story. Colt braced a hand on the truck, aiming to look like his world wasn't spinning in circles. "What brings you out here?"

"I'm your backup."

Colt's eyes narrowed. "I thought everybody who was anybody was occupied elsewhere." He winced. That definitely sounded bad, like Ethan was as much of an outcast as Colt.

It must have shown on his face, because Ethan grinned. "I'm definitely an 'anybody,' yet here I am. Vance figured we had enough manpower on that whole 'elsewhere' thing, especially after it became clear tonight that we need eyes on both Segovias. Now that the kid has a definite inroad to the cartel, we want him alive and we want him and his sister safe. If we can bring down more of the cartel in the process—"

"Then so much the better."

"I think that's the thought process, yeah." Ethan drummed his fingers on the door, staring at the front of Danielle's apartment building. The way he refused to meet Colt's eye, there must be something else.

"What's going on? You act like you're afraid I'm going to shoot the messenger and the messenger's you."

Grinning, Ethan shot Colt a glance, then turned serious. "This is what makes you a good Ranger, Blackthorn. That gut of yours. You don't miss a thing."

Ethan could believe that all he wanted, but Colt knew the truth. His gut had only gotten him into trouble lately.

"Vance wanted me to tell you something in person. He thought a phone call would be…" Ethan waved his hand as though the gesture should explain everything in the world.

It had to be about Carmen. They finally had word about Carmen. There was nothing else that would make the major believe in-person news was better than a phone call…

Unless another of their team had gone missing. Colt planted his feet and waited, determined not to waver no matter what Ethan said next.

"Trevor Street heard from an informant he's been cultivating." Ethan worked his jaw back and forth, his fingers still drumming on the truck door. "Apparently, right around the time Carmen vanished, Garcia put out some feelers to his own intel network, found out Carmen's with us."

Dropping his head back, Colt stared at the sky. So

Garcia knew. He'd figured out Carmen wasn't on the up and up. "Street's guy say if he had any leads on where she might be?"

Ethan shook his head. "Not a word."

"If Carmen's as smart as I think she is, she's hiding. We've got to believe this is one of those times when no news is a good thing. If Garcia had managed to find her… Well, he'd be parading that out in the open like a trophy. He'd want the world to know." It would be foolish, parading a dead Ranger out in the open and admitting to the murder, but it would also be just like Garcia. "Look at what he did to Kylie Perry's informant. Left her right where she'd be found with that *T* on her forehead." *Traitor*. Garcia believed in sending messages, and if he had Carmen Alvarez, there was no way he'd keep silent.

Unless he was holding on to her for future leverage. If that was the case, there was no telling what torture she was enduring now.

FIFTEEN

Standing in front of her open spice cabinet, Danielle stared at the contents, hardly seeing them.

Christmas Eve.

She was *this close* to saying, "Bah! Humbug!" and going back to bed.

Might as well. It wasn't like she could dash out to the grocery store for the fixings for Christmas dinner. She definitely couldn't go to the Mission and hand out toys to the kids. She was trapped here, in the apartment, with her brother and a man she couldn't stop thinking about.

The year her parents had died had been the worst holiday season of her life. She'd forced her way through for Justin, but there had been no true spirit of rejoicing to the season. She'd been angry with God, angry with herself, angry in general that first Christmas. For the better part of six months, she'd been certain she'd never get over her anger. But then, when Justin was at a church lock-in one Friday night near Easter, she'd finally been alone for the first time in their new-to-them apartment. In the silence of late night, fretting over all of the horrible things she'd been certain would happen to Justin while he wasn't safely under their roof, Danielle had cracked. For the better part of an hour, she'd stood in the living room and railed at God for the injustice of losing her parents, her future…

When she'd broken down, lying across her bed and venting her anger in a storm of tears, the film washed away until she could see the world clearly again. She could feel her heart beating for the first time since the phone call came and changed her life forever.

For every year since, Christmas and even Easter had carried a whole new meaning. She'd been able to sense God's grace, love and peace like never before.

Until this year.

"What's got you so spun up?" Colt's voice came from behind her, near the bar. When Danielle turned, he had taken a spot on one of the stools.

His brown eyes sparked with an expectation she couldn't quite puzzle out. His hair was still damp from his run home to take a shower and grab clean clothes. His skin still had a slight flush from the cold that was strong enough to feel like Christmas weather, a rarity in El Paso.

The whole package was enough to make her want to lean across the counter and pick up the kiss they'd dropped the night before. But after hearing about his brother, his push-pull with her had her thinking it might be better to let him be, even if it made her heart ache. "I was just thinking. A few years ago, I was completely worried about what could happen to Justin at a church lock-in surrounded by chaperones and friends he'd known since preschool. Now…" She swiped her hair back from her face. "Now the danger can walk right into our living room."

Colt leaned his forearms on the bar and started to say something, but Justin wandered in, his hair rumpled, his T-shirt full of wrinkles and a yawn still stretching his mouth. He stopped when he saw Danielle in the kitchen. "Cookies?" His voice arched up the way it used to when he was a kid. "Are you finally going to make cookies? I figured you'd given up this year."

The way his eyes widened with an almost childlike expectation grabbed her by the heart. Yes, this year was different. Yes, the future was uncertain and, right now, terrifying. But her fears didn't have to dictate her brother's life any more than hers. She'd been selfish these past few days, mentally boxing up Christmas, thinking only of her own thoughts and feelings. All along, her brother had needed something only she could give him.

A sister's love…

And Christmas cookies.

Colt looked over his shoulder at Justin, then made a big show of checking the heavy black wristwatch he seemed to never take off. "It's after eleven in the morning. You always crawl out of bed at the crack of noon and demand cookies?"

"This is early for a non-school day." Danielle slid a cookie sheet from the drawer beneath the oven and tried to find the joy in making cookies from her mother's recipe. It had brought comfort every other year. Maybe it would work now, too.

"I only get up early for Christmas Day." Justin straddled the bar stool next to Colt's. "You haven't ever eaten good cookies until you've eaten Dani's ginger snaps. Oh, and you have to have eggnog." He perked up. "We have eggnog, right?"

With a quick glance at Colt, Danielle turned her back on the cabinet and faced her brother, hands on hips, a mock glare drawing her eyebrows together. "And just when do you think I've had time to—"

"In the fridge."

Hands falling from her hips to hang at her sides, Danielle shifted her attention to Colt. "I'm sorry?"

"There's eggnog in the fridge."

Danielle walked backward the two steps to the refrigerator, her eyes never leaving Colt until she pulled the door open to reveal a fully-stocked-for-Christmas fridge. Eggnog, ham from that place with the amazing candied glaze, prepared side dishes and the ingredients for more…

Tears pushed against the backs of her eyes as she shut the door, her gaze glued to the candle-shaped magnet from the church. If she turned around now, she might cry real tears over a fridge full of food.

No, not food. Over a man who had somehow managed to see into her heart and make her Christmas wishes come true.

When she'd composed herself, she pulled in a deep breath and worked up the courage to look Colt square in the eye. "Thank you." The words seemed too quiet to make it across the small kitchen to him.

They must have been exactly loud enough, because he smiled and tipped his head toward her.

With a mighty groan, Justin shoved away from the counter. "You two are disgusting. I'm going to take a shower. Call me when the cookies are ready."

He was halfway up the hall before Danielle realized her mouth was hanging open. She shut it, heat flushing her cheeks. That boy... If he was still eight years old, she'd put him and his smart mouth in time-out.

Colt was probably mortified.

But no, Colt was chuckling.

Now would be the perfect time for him to get up, round the counter and kiss her again like he had the day before. The most perfectly wonderful time.

Instead, he stayed where he was, drumming his fingers on the counter, an action that seemed to be his nervous habit of choice. "You know, we haven't really talked about tomorrow yet."

Tomorrow. Was that a metaphor for what happened next for the two of them? They needed to discuss it.

"Tomorrow's Christmas and I have no idea what you do. I mean, how does your day normally look? I tried to guess what you guys might want for dinner, but... If you need anything else, I can have it delivered. And I can make myself scarce tomorrow while—"

"Stay." The word came out more forcefully than she'd intended. As in, she hadn't intended it to come out at all. But the idea of Christmas without Colt was suddenly all wrong. He belonged here.

Either he felt the same way or she was going to have a world of hurt coming while she dealt with the fact that he didn't. Danielle sunk her teeth into her bottom lip and turned away from him, reaching for the mixing bowl. She shouldn't have put herself out there that way. He'd think she was chasing him. A guy like Colt didn't—

Warm hands rested on her shoulders, and Colt's forehead pressed the back of her head. "I will." The two small words shot electricity down her spine, which erupted into dancing butterflies in her stomach.

Danielle moved to turn toward him but Colt stopped her with a firm pressure on her shoulders. "We need to talk about…" He inhaled and backed away from her. "We need to talk first."

Those dreaded, awful words nobody wanted to hear. He was going to tell her she was simply a part of the job. That they could only be friends. That once this was all over, he'd be on his way and maybe they'd run into each other someday.

She'd beat him to the punch. Sliding the mixing bowl onto the counter, she lifted her chin. "I know. Yesterday was a fluke. A moment that shouldn't have happened. Got it."

But she didn't. Deep in her heart, she knew this was rapidly becoming more than a one-kiss deal for her.

"That's not what…"

Slipping sideways away from him, Danielle stuck her head in the fridge, reaching for the eggs. She needed something, anything to do with her hands, some place to keep her eyes so they didn't wander to his. "You have a job to do. I have a brother to raise. We're both… Well, at least I'm emotional right now. It's no wonder things got out of hand. And that's all it was—just an emotional reaction. Nothing more."

"So that's what this is." His voice was hard, a cold thread she'd never heard before running through it. "Emotions. Fear."

"Nothing more."

"Fine. Then tomorrow—" He stopped abruptly as his phone buzzed on the kitchen counter. He grabbed it and muttered something under his breath as he read the screen, then stalked toward the door. "I have to step outside. Austin wants to talk to me. The mission the team is on got moved up. I'll be right downstairs if you need anything." He slammed out the door before she could respond.

Danielle leaned against the counter, fingers wrapped around the edges, and prayed for sanity. She also prayed that, when this was all over, both Justin and her heart would survive.

Colt hit the bottom of the stairs and scanned the parking lot out of habit. Over the past few days, he'd learned which cars belonged and which ones didn't. The only ones out of place right now were Hilliard's vehicle on the other side of the parking lot, where he was laying low, and Austin's pickup, sitting two spaces away from the foot of the stairs.

Frankly, he was a little grateful for Austin's call. He needed a breather from the heaviness in the apartment.

From the woman who'd turned cold on him.

So Danielle thought what was happening between them was just an overly emotional response to the chaos swirling around her. Maybe that was all it was for her, but his whole life had been chaos, and he'd never felt about any woman like he did about Danielle. Even Carmen Alvarez, who was one of his closest friends, who'd gone through training with him, hadn't caught his attention the way Danielle had.

Colt stopped in midstride. As dangerous as it was, he had to admit it. He loved Danielle Segovia. Impossible after such a short time, but true. The way her words had sliced through his skin and ripped apart his heart this morning was the proof. If he looked down at his chest, he'd probably see blood.

Colt glanced at Austin, who watched him with a furrowed brow. In the passenger seat, Kylie studied him as only a woman could. She was picking up his thoughts for sure. He'd have to be careful.

Austin lowered his window, looking beat-down tired. Even though his damp hair said he'd recently had a shower and he'd changed into civilian clothes, both Kylie and he held that grungy air that said they'd been on stakeout too long and had fought the enemy too hard.

Colt straightened, on high alert.

Kylie smiled grimly and leaned forward to get a good look at him around Austin.

"How'd it go?" Colt was half glad he hadn't known in advance that the mission was moved up. He'd have added that to his reasons not to sleep last night.

"Identified a fruit truck when it came across the border. We tailed them and took them down about a mile in. Every piece of fruit in the truck was hollowed out and packed with drugs. Even the crates they were shipped in were modified for stealth packaging." Kylie shook her head, toying with the pocket on her sweat-shirt. "We ended up in a shootout. Two tangos escaped, but we got the driver. He's being interrogated."

"Anybody hurt?" He glanced at Austin, who shook his head once.

Kylie puffed out a breath, her eyes clouding. "Border Patrol agent. New guy. Took one in the thigh but he should be okay."

One of her people. Sometimes, the bullets hit a little too close to home.

Austin reached for Kylie's hand and squeezed it. The shadows beneath his blue eyes spoke of his weariness. "How's Danielle?"

That question was locked and loaded, even if Austin

didn't realize it. "Fine now. Had a scuffle last night." He ran down the series of events from the night before, leaving out the kiss that definitely *should* have happened, even if Danielle didn't believe it yet.

The way Kylie was watching him, it was obvious she knew he was leaving something unsaid. She started to speak, but Austin didn't seem to notice and cut her off.

"Between your captures and the driver, Vance believes we have a shot at some decent intel on Garcia's organization. Unfortunately, nobody's talking yet. They're more afraid of what Garcia can do to them than of what we can. The threat of life in prison isn't all that scary when the alternative is torture then death."

It wasn't unusual for the kingpin's people to choose silence over his wrath. Eventually though, they'd get someone willing to talk. They had to.

Kylie let go of Austin's hand and dragged her hands down her face, rubbing at the lines of weariness etched there. This mission was taking a toll on the entire team. "DEA is estimating the street value of that truck is enough to put a serious hurt on Garcia's finances— and he's got to be feeling the strain on his supply this side of the border."

Good. Sooner or later, Rio Garcia would figure out he couldn't do business here anymore. DEA, Border Patrol and the Texas Rangers were proving they had him in an ever-tightening fist.

The problem was, being trapped might just make the cartel leader kick harder.

"Vance wants you on high alert, though. He's going to keep you inside and one of us outside at all times. He's afraid our success in this raid is going to make

Garcia ten times madder. If he still believes Danielle is his sister, hiding away the stash he now needs desperately, he's going to come at her harder than ever," Austin said. "We picked up some intel that says his next attack against her could possibly be in person. Garcia's getting desperate. He's out for blood, coming full force after his sister and shaking down his whole organization to weed out informants."

"It might be time to move Danielle and Justin into protective custody." She'd balk, especially on Christmas Eve, but the time to be sentimental had ended. Her life was in deeper jeopardy than ever.

"Vance said the same thing, but he said you're unsure she'll agree and we really can't force her." Exhaling loudly, Austin glanced at Kylie before leaning closer to Colt. "You get the latest word on Carmen?"

"Hilliard told me."

Austin scrubbed his hand down the day-old beard on his cheek. "Carmen's smart. She'll make her way back. If Garcia had her, we'd know by now."

"Especially as mad as he is," Kylie said, her expression dark. "I just feel like… I mean, I've been praying for her but…"

"But 'wherever two or more are gathered,' right?" Austin laid a hand on her shoulder.

Colt nodded slowly. It might be that praying for Carmen was the best thing they could do for her.

Laying his hand on Colt's shoulder, Austin prayed, thanking God for the safety of their team, for healing of the injured Border Patrol agent and for Carmen's safety.

Silently, Colt added Danielle and Justin to the prayer. As they broke apart, he felt a lightness in his chest and across his shoulders, as though he'd been hauling around a rucksack that was too heavy. For the first time in years, he truly believed God had heard and would answer. Maybe, just maybe, Danielle's faith was reminding him what kind of God they truly served.

He bit back a smile. Maybe he should try finally telling God he was angry about Caleb's death. Would that give him this same sense of liberation?

No, Colt wasn't quite ready for that yet. He wasn't totally sure God wouldn't throw a bolt of lightning his way for following up his first real prayer in years with a declaration of anger.

"You need anything?" Austin asked. "I'm supposed to go home and get a quick rest then come back and spell Hilliard out here in the parking lot."

"We're good." He was anxious to get back upstairs. Even the peace of praying wasn't enough to keep him from wanting to be right next to Danielle. But first… "Actually, can you do me a quick solid and stop at the grocery store on your way back? Her brother mentioned wanting eggnog this morning and they have some, but not enough to satisfy a teenaged boy for long."

Kylie's eyebrow rose, and Austin gave him a crooked grin. "Never figured you as one that would go soft, Blackthorn."

"What's that supposed—"

"Colt!" His name blasted from above, a shriek of panic.

His heart fell to his shoes. He was halfway up the stairs when he heard Kylie and Austin pounding up the cement steps behind him.

Danielle stood at the railing, shaking and pale.

Colt grabbed her by the shoulders, forcing her to

look at him. What had happened while he was standing right outside her door? Nobody had come by them. "What's wrong?"

"Colt." His name choked out on a sob. "Justin's gone."

SIXTEEN

Danielle stood in front of her bed and stared at the empty backpack in front of her. Her brother was gone, using his bed sheets to climb out of his second-story window while she and Colt were only a room away. It wasn't possible. He'd been warned to stay put, to not leave. Had his entire apology, his begging Colt for help, been an act?

Colt had sent her into her bedroom while Austin and Kylie raced back down the stairs to search the apartment complex. In the living room, Colt paced and talked on the phone, calling for backup, his words too low for her to hear.

The backpack on her bed spurred her into motion, but she wasn't sure where to start. What did someone pack when they expected to be kidnapped by a cartel leader?

Her mind was completely out of control if she was looking for a way to make this even remotely amusing. Her baby brother was missing, in the hands of the Garcia cartel. The message on her new cell phone held an unquestionable demand: If you want our brother to be safe, Adriana, you will contact this number and meet me. Alone. Your life for his.

Our brother? It had to be a typo. If it wasn't, then in Rio Garcia's twisted mind, Danielle was Adriana and Justin was somehow related to both of them. That didn't even make sense—he must truly be a madman. Every time she thought the nightmare couldn't get any worse...

Hands trembling, she brushed her hair out of her face, then shoved the bright red backpack to the center of the bed and dropped to her knees on the floor, laying her head on the quilt her mother had sewn shortly before Danielle was born. What would her mother say now if she knew how Danielle had failed to protect Justin?

Tears soaked the bright fabric as she laid out her fears before her God. There were no spoken words, only cries from her heart that defied words and poured out in emotions she couldn't fully express. A sense of solace swept over her, like a candle lighting the way through the darkness of her fear. Finally, the words came to her. *God, help me. Save Justin. Save us. Please.* The words swam over and over in varying order. She couldn't do this alone. She needed God now more than ever.

"Danielle." Colt's voice came from the doorway, then he knelt beside her, pulling her closer.

A rush of trust washed over her. Instinctively, she felt that Colt would handle this. He'd take care of them.

But then fear took over again. Was there anything he could do to save them all now?

Danielle cried into his chest as his hands stroked her hair and he whispered words she couldn't quite capture. But the words didn't really matter. For the moment, his presence was enough.

When the storm subsided, Colt helped Danielle to her feet and held her to him. His kiss was a breath against her hair. "I've got the entire team in motion, but before they get here, you need to tell me exactly what happened in the two minutes I was downstairs."

Sniffling, Danielle backed away and swiped at her cheeks. As much comfort as Colt was, they didn't have time for this. They had to search, to track down Justin before the worst happened. "We have to go find him. We can't stand here talking."

"I get that. I do." Colt's dark eyes scanned hers. "Believe me. But we can't go running off with the gun half-cocked. We need to know how long he's been gone. It will give us a clue where to look. Half of my team is en route, waiting for us to tell them which direction to take. The other half is already working their contacts and hitting the streets. Talk to me, then we'll do whatever it takes to bring Justin home." He dipped his head, his voice dropping along with it. "I promise."

Danielle nodded once, slowly. If anyone understood the urgency of the situation, Colt did. As much as she wanted to run for the border to turn herself over to the cartel, Colt was right. This had to be done systematically and thoughtfully, even as her emotions screamed for action.

Pulling in a deep breath, Danielle fought for focus. "I don't know how long he's been gone. I haven't seen him since he went to his room earlier. It had to have happened while we were both in here. A couple of minutes after you went outside, I got a text from a number I don't recognize. It told me I can have my brother back when I give myself up. I ran to Justin's room..." Panic dug into her chest and clawed its way toward her stomach. She had to wake up from this nightmare, because this couldn't truly be happening to them. "His window was open. His phone was on the bed. And he was gone. That's when I yelled for you."

"This is my fault." He ground out the words, then his eyebrows drew together and his lips tightened. "We can't track him by his cell phone if it's not on him. Where is it? If nothing else, we can find out who he was talking to. It might give us a lead."

Reaching above her head, Danielle pulled a cell phone from the nightstand and handed it to Colt. He pressed the screen and muttered something she couldn't understand, his face tightening. "It's locked. Do you know the code?" When Danielle shook her head, he turned toward the door. "Hilliard!"

Footsteps pounded up the short hallway and a guy a few years older than Colt appeared in the doorway. Colt tossed him the cell phone. "Get that to Jenny and have her work her brand of awesome on it. It's Justin's. Oh, and call her and tell her I'm texting her some info to trace. Someone's contacted Danielle on her phone, too."

"On it." The other man was gone as quickly as he'd appeared, and the slam of the front door shook the apartment.

"Where's your cell?" Colt was all business again. He was no longer the man who'd held her close and comforted her only a moment before. He was the Ranger who was going to save her brother.

Sliding the phone from her pocket, Danielle passed it to him without a word. He'd become a stranger, but a welcome one. This was the man who'd interrogated her at the hospital, only this time, his ire was aimed at someone else, his drive directed at helping her.

"Password?"

She gave it to him and he keyed it in, scanning the screen before his expression darkened. His eyes narrowed, and he glanced at the bed before he snatched the backpack from its place. "Is that what this is about? Were you packing a bag to go turn yourself over? Are you seriously thinking this is some sort of vacation?" His voice was low but it held the force of a shout. "Absolutely not. You are not trading yourself for your brother."

Cold fury fueled by terror shuddered in her stomach and radiated outward into her limbs. "I have to."

"Do you realize what he's asking of you?" Colt dragged his hand across his head and paced toward the door. "He's not asking for Danielle Segovia to turn herself in. He's asking for his sister. Are you Adriana Garcia?"

Stomach clinching, Danielle sank her teeth into her lower lip. Colt's back was to her, but he might as well be shaking her shoulders.

Turning toward her, he strode closer. "Are you?"

"You know I'm not."

"Then what exactly do you think Rio Garcia will do to you *and* Justin when he figures that out? Give you a high five and tell you to have a nice day, that he's sorry for the inconvenience? No way. Danielle, he will kill you both. On the spot. No questions, no arguments. He's killed people for a whole lot less than not being his sister."

Danielle quaked from the inside out, both from the look on Colt's face and the fear of what Rio Garcia might do to Justin if she didn't give herself up. "You don't get it. Justin's not your brother."

Colt drew back as though she'd struck him, then

glanced over her shoulder toward her window. "He might as well be." He tossed the backpack onto the bed and laid his hands on her shoulders with a gentleness that surprised her. "You have an entire company of Rangers looking for the man who has your brother. They're the best of the best. And you have me. I promised I'd keep you safe, and Justin is a part of that promise. But you have to do what I say, and you have to promise me that you won't run off and do something foolish like giving yourself over to Garcia's men."

Danielle stared into his eyes, trying not to flinch. She couldn't make that promise. If she was certain the Rangers wouldn't be able to save her brother in time and it came down to her life or Justin's, she had no doubt what she'd do, and lying to Colt right now wouldn't make a difference.

"Danielle…" His voice was ragged. "If you can't make that promise I'll have Kylie escort you to headquarters and put you in protective custody." She started to speak, but his fingers tightened on her shoulders. "I can't do my job if I'm worried you're going to take off on me. Please. Promise me." Fear flashed behind the steel in his eyes.

The same fear her own soul felt thinking about her brother. She couldn't put Colt through this kind of pain and terror. Tears drying on her cheeks, she nodded once.

He exhaled slowly and pressed a kiss to her forehead. "Okay. Now, I think I know where your brother is."

SEVENTEEN

Danielle sat at a table in the team room at headquarters and buried her face in her hands. From the hallway, muffled voices floated to her, but none of the sounds gelled into words she could understand through the ringing in her ears.

Colt had been so certain he knew where her brother was. He'd packed her off to headquarters to wait with him for word, and they'd spent nearly two hours pacing in the team room, listening to radio traffic and waiting.

The team had come back empty-handed.

She'd argued then, desperate to go back to her apartment in case Justin managed to escape and make his way home. The discussion had escalated to her yelling at Colt, crying and blaming him. If he hadn't left them alone... If he hadn't walked into her store in the first place...

Warm tears leaked between her fingers. No, that was wrong. If he hadn't shown up when he did, she'd be dead already and Justin would be alone.

None of this was Colt's fault. All she'd needed was someone to take out her frustration on. Did he realize that? He'd walked out of the room, his back straight and shoulders squared.

All she'd wanted was to call him back, especially when he'd silently pulled the door shut behind him. If he'd have slammed it, the sound couldn't have been any more condemning. She'd wrecked him. After everything he'd shared about his brother, she'd heaped guilt on him, blaming him for Justin, tearing his heart open.

A warm hand rested lightly on her back. Danielle jumped and lifted her head, her heart rising, but she sank into the seat when she realized the hand belonged to Jenny and not Colt.

Jenny pressed a wad of crumpled paper towels into Danielle's hand then settled into a chair beside her. "Sorry it's not nice, soft tissue. That was the best I could scrounge up around this place. You'd think we could do better than that."

Danielle gave her a weak smile, pressing the rough paper towel to her eyes. "Thanks." She pulled in a deep breath and dared to ask the question she'd been afraid to voice since they arrived. "Any more word on my brother?"

Jenny hesitated, then shook her head. "I'm still trying to crack the password into his phone. Those things are encrypted better than you'd think. My team's on it. We'll get into it. In the meantime, we're combing through Justin's phone records to see if we can trace any calls or texts. We won't be able to know what was said, but we'll at least be able to know where the contact originated."

Danielle stared at her hands, shredding the paper towel and laying the thin wisps on the table in front of her. She'd spent a few minutes with Jenny's team, trying to puzzle out what her brother's password could be, but nothing she could think of had worked. If they tried and failed too many times, they could be locked out for good.

Her fingers were cold and stiff as she pulled the paper towel apart. Jenny was nice. Under different circumstances, they might even be friends, but Danielle really needed Colt right now. She should go find him. Apologize. Try to make things right...

Reaching across the small space between them, Jenny laid her hand over Danielle's, pulling away the shredded fibers and piling them on the table. "I know this isn't easy, but we're all doing the best we can." She squeezed Danielle's fingers. "Even Colt."

"Where is he?"

"In Major Vance's office. They're working with our intel analysts, trying to find your brother. And they will. Our guys are good. And Colt is determined."

The truth squeezed around Danielle's heart. Colt was determined. It was clear from the way he'd behaved all along that he cared for her...and for Justin. What had she done to repay him? Stabbed him in the heart. "I hurt him."

"You did." Jenny's voice was matter-of-fact, no accusation. No anger. Just truth. She sat back and placed both hands on the table in front of her, staring at the wall across the room. "But I understand. Deep inside, Colt does, too. You're scared. You're worried. You lashed out. He's done the same." She sniffed bitterly. "Just ask Brent McCord. Those two came to the Rangers about the same time. They were..." Jenny shook her head, glanced at Danielle, then turned back to the wall. "Never mind."

Danielle had gathered over the past few days that Brent and Colt had been friends at one point but were now cold to each other. Maybe that was Colt's way, freezing out anyone who got too close. Maybe her outburst at the house had just helped him on his way out the door.

"Thing about Colt is, I've never seen him act like this." Seeming to read Danielle's thoughts, Jenny turned to face her. "He's always been one of those guys who don't get involved. He does the job and gets out. Nothing rattles him. Maybe it's his military training. Maybe it's whatever happened to him when he was younger that he never talks about. But no matter what the case, he manages to keep this professional detachment around him." Jenny's gaze pinned hers. "This time's different. He's destroyed over your brother. He's aching over you." She smiled and shook her head. "And the way he was here with you when y'all stopped by the other day? The hand on your back as you walked out the door? The way he was watching you when he thought nobody could see him? Danielle, Colt's a gentlemen, but with you? That's a whole lot more. That's a man who's finally had the shell around his heart cracked."

A whisper of joyful expectation ran along Danielle's arms. Shoving the emotion away, she stood and walked to the door where Colt had exited earlier. "I can't think about that right now." There was too much else to worry about tonight.

Justin was missing because of her. Until he was safe again, there was no future to consider. Without her only surviving family, her future was bleak anyway. She needed Justin to be safe more than she needed to be safe herself. If she lost him… "I want to trade myself for my brother."

"Absolutely not." The voice over her shoulder whipped into the room, hard and angry. Danielle whirled to face it.

Colt stood in the doorway at the front of the room, stance wide, arms crossed. His pistol was holstered at his hip and his gaze was hard. "You cannot trade yourself for Justin. Rio Garcia will—"

"Will what? Kill me? He'll do the same thing to Justin if I don't turn myself over to him, and then he'll come for me again. Justin's dead if I don't do something soon. He's already dead if Garcia finds out I'm here with you instead of—"

"Danielle, you're the one who's dead if you let Garcia get his hands on you. You're not who he wants. Nothing's going to change that."

"Then use me as bait." Danielle strode closer to Colt, stopping only a few feet away from him. Determination flowed through her veins. She'd do whatever it took to save her brother. The consequences could be sorted out later. "Let me tell Garcia I'll only turn myself over to him if he lets Justin free at the same time. It will flush him out for you and you can take him into custody while you save Justin and me."

"No."

As far as Danielle was concerned, it was the only way. They were at a standstill without access to Justin's phone, and even that access wouldn't guarantee them answers. This was their best chance.

Although it broke her heart to buck him, Danielle went toe to toe with Colt, lifting her chin to stare him in the eye. "Then you'd better be prepared to lock me up, because the minute your back is turned, I'm gone, alone, to rescue my brother."

"You can't possibly be considering this." Colt paced from one side of the team room to the other as Jenny fitted a small tracker into a seam close to the knee of Danielle's blue jeans.

Fear he hadn't felt since the night Caleb died pumped through him, pounding in his head. It blended with anger to make his ears roar and his vision blur.

His team was out of control. Common sense had flown out the window with the opportunity to draw in a big score like Rio Garcia. They were putting Danielle in danger for a plan that could easily fail.

Garcia had eyes everywhere and was bound to know she was here with the Rangers, was certain to know this was a trap. Every one of the people standing in this room could be dead before morning.

"This could be a setup. Garcia could know exactly who Danielle is. This could be about us and not her. He could be baiting us into going to this exchange and waiting to ambush us."

"That's not what our intel says." Brent McCord sat on a table, his hands braced beside his thighs. "All of the chatter we've picked up shows no indication he's currently planning anything against us or Border Patrol."

Colt wanted to plant his fist in Brent's nose. Ever since Colt had taken issues with Brent's steadfast belief in Adriana Garcia's innocence, it seemed they agreed on nothing, that Brent automatically argued Colt down on everything he said. He started to give Brent a huge chunk of his mind but stopped. It would make him seem petty and childish, and he was sick of fighting like children, especially when so much was at stake.

Watching as the team prepped Danielle for the faux exchange and coached her on what to say for the phone call to Garcia's men, Colt realized a little bit of what Brent might be feeling. He didn't buy that you could know someone after a two-minute meeting, the way Brent claimed he knew Adriana, but he was certain about one thing...he'd also never believed that love came as quickly as it had with Danielle. When she'd railed at him this afternoon, unleashing her frustration and pain on him, the cut had been quick and harsh.

It had confirmed every feeling he'd fought against. Even right now, knowing she was walking into the kind of danger that even trained agents had died in, he knew more than ever.... He loved her.

He'd take a bullet for her.

And for Justin.

When this was over, he'd tell her. Truthfully, if he could get her alone now, he'd tell her. Maybe it would change her mind and get her off this incredibly foolish idea that she could somehow save the world by turning herself over to a killer.

"Call it off." Colt turned to Ethan Hilliard, who was acting as the ranking member on this mission. "It's a bad idea." He glanced at Danielle, who turned her back to him when she noticed he was watching.

She had the support of his entire team. She didn't need him.

Hilliard shook his head. "This is the best shot we have of rescuing Justin Segovia and of nabbing Garcia once and for all." With a pointed look at Danielle, Ethan clamped a hand on Colt's shoulder and directed him to the hallway, dropping his voice to a low rumble. "She'll be safe. We'll be right on her the whole time. You're a tactical genius, Blackthorn. You've been on ops like this a dozen times. You know how it works. If you weren't in love with this girl, you'd see this plan is the best course of action."

"I'm n—" Colt clamped his mouth shut. He wouldn't deny it, not even for the sake of the mission.

Ethan almost smiled. The corner of his lip twitched. "Smart man." The amusement vanished as fast as it had appeared. He leaned back to check the action inside the team room, then looked at Colt. "Look, we've asked for an SRT to be on standby."

Colt exhaled as some of the tension in his shoulders eased. The special response teams were made up of elite members of the Rangers, Texas Highway Patrol and the Criminal Investigations Division. Trained for crisis situations—including hostages and barricaded suspects—an SRT would provide much-needed protection if Garcia somehow managed to snatch Danielle.

"Take a breather, Blackthorn. Say a prayer. The Segovias will be fine. Trust your team. They trust you."

Ethan disappeared into the team room again before Colt could respond.

If his team trusted him, they had a crazy way of acting like it. Putting him on guard duty, shutting him out of mission planning...

Tapping the back of his head against the wall, Colt turned his face to the ceiling and grimaced. This was a giant pity party. He sounded like his fifteen-year-old cousin when her friends went to the mall without her.

Scrubbing his cheeks with his palms, he closed his eyes. What had seemed futile only a few days ago now became his refuge, thanks to the faith of Danielle and his team. *Lord, I know You have Danielle in Your hands just like I know You have Carmen. Help me. Trusting You isn't easy after losing Caleb.*

A light shove on his arm jerked him around. Ethan was leaning out the door. "She's making the call, and she's asking for you."

Okay, then. This was happening. Colt cast another quick glance upward and surrendered as he walked into the room. God was going to have to handle this. He couldn't.

Danielle stood at one of the tables holding her phone. Other members of the team were scattered around the room, waiting. When she saw him, she smiled grimly and held out her hand.

In spite of all he'd done to shove her away, she still needed him.

Somehow, it made him feel about two feet taller.

He grasped her hand and pulled her close to his side. "You can do this."

Relief washed over her features at his acceptance of her actions, and Colt felt shame heat the back of his neck. He'd been fighting what needed to be done, leaving Danielle conflicted. He should have come around sooner.

With a deep breath, she pressed the screen on her phone and pulled it to her ear. From her office across the hall, Jenny could pick up every word via wireless and would work at tracing whoever answered on the other end.

Colt was close enough to hear the voice when it answered. *"¿Estás solo?"*

Are you alone?

Danielle's fingers tightened on Colt's. She swallowed hard and her voice shook, forcing Colt to dig his fingers into his thigh to keep from taking the phone and dealing with this himself. *"Si. Mi hermano—"*

The male voice spoke in rapid Spanish, the sound too muffled for Colt to pick up more than a few words.

Pressing in tightly to his side, Danielle seemed to force out the words the Rangers had given her to speak. Her voice fell in a soft, lyrical Spanish that Colt would have loved to drown in had it not been for the situation. "I only turn myself in to Rio. No one else."

There was a quick flurry of words from the other side, angry and loud, before the call ended.

Danielle pressed the screen and handed the phone to Colt, then melted in his arms, trembling. "He's coming."

Colt pulled her close, holding her to his chest. He shut out everyone else in the room, refusing to care what anyone else thought. Danielle needed him, and he was going to do what he could to be there for her. Pressing a kiss to the side of her head, he glanced up when Jenny came in the room carrying a tablet.

"The requested location is an abandoned warehouse near the river. Place is popular with drug mules and human smugglers. It's a known locale that DEA has eyes on already, so you need to be careful. Garcia likely knows the place is being watched and will be on high alert, but he's probably choosing it for that reason, because it's the last place anybody would expect him to be. Risky, but the payoff's huge for him. He must be close by, because the exchange is in an hour."

"That's not much time to get into place." Hilliard took charge as Danielle pulled away from Colt and tugged at the hem of her shirt. "We have to move now."

EIGHTEEN

Crouched deep in the cover of abandoned shipping containers, Colt shivered as the wind tunneled through the narrow aisles, whipping against him with a cold fury. He trained his eyes on the back of the warehouse, where a streetlamp cast weak light over a neglected parking lot.

Stationed around the building, five other Rangers kept watch. Less than half a mile away, the special response team was geared up and waiting, insurance against a worst-case scenario.

Colt's earpiece was silent. This mission was too important to risk nonessential communication being picked up by someone on the outside.

The Rangers had crept in one by one, taking their places under cover of darkness as Danielle waited to drive up in her own vehicle, trailed at a distance by Austin Brewer.

Colt's muscles were tense, ready to leap at the first sign of trouble. He'd been separated from Danielle at headquarters without the opportunity to tell her he was praying for her and that he loved her. As he'd made his way across town to the rendezvous point, he'd prayed and warred with himself, fighting to wrestle his emotions into a box that would let him do his job and keep him from thinking about the fact that the failure of this mission meant death for someone he cared about.

Tactical box, Blackthorn. In the army, he'd learned to divide himself into pieces, separating the man and his emotions from the job and his mind. Tonight called for that detachment more than ever.

He scanned the back of the warehouse, narrowing his eyes as yet another short line of people made their way up from the river into the shadows of the long, low building. Kylie was closer and was tasked with watching faces, keeping eyes wide open for Garcia or any of his known bodyguards. Inside the building, Hilliard and McCord were in position, waiting.

At first, Colt had wondered why Garcia would choose to meet at such a highly trafficked area. Since they'd arrived and watched dozens of people flow in and out of the abandoned building, there was no doubt. Every great tactician knew there was great cover to be found in blending in with others. Dozens of people had come in and out of the warehouse since Colt had taken his position, smuggling who knew what. The warehouse was practically a shopping mall for all things illegal. With this kind of traffic, Garcia could slip in completely unnoticed, one man in a sea of faces. And if there was any kind of violence or confrontation, so what? No one here would ever report it to the authorities.

It was no wonder DEA hadn't yet shut this place down. It was probably their greatest gold mine. They likely had informants of all kinds flowing through here. If he wasn't on the most important mission of his life, Colt would likely be cultivating some himself.

It was a huge bonus for law enforcement that men like Rio Garcia felt safe enough to come here. Holding out on raiding this place to take down the small prizes made it a false refuge for criminals, one the good guys could charge into when a big fish made a rare appearance.

Like tonight.

An older gray SUV slipped around the warehouse, bouncing along the cracked pavement, and slid to a halt near a back door, so close that when the vehicle's door opened, the occupants had to squeeze out through a narrow space between the SUV and the wall.

Colt straightened and lifted his binoculars. The first man to exit stood between the end of the SUV and the door, blocking Colt's view of the vehicle's remaining occupants as they scurried from the back seat into the warehouse.

But he recognized the face of the man facing him. The Rangers, DEA, Border Patrol... They had all studied Garcia's known bodyguards and, while this one's name was unknown, the long scar across his forehead was unmistakable. Around Echo Company, he'd earned the nickname Frankenstein, after the Boris Karloff version of the character who bore a similar scar.

The appearance of Frankenstein almost definitely meant Garcia was in that vehicle, that he'd kept his word and had shown up for Danielle personally. Still, they couldn't go in yet, not until they had confirmation. To jump now meant a high risk for failure, and if this was a setup and they were wrong, then they'd likely never get another shot...

And Justin would be dead.

Colt inhaled through his nose and exhaled though his

mouth, centering himself on the mission. *Focus.* This wasn't personal. It couldn't be.

Headlights swept around the back of the building and Danielle's small two-door came into view. She had to be terrified making this approach by herself, even though the Rangers had wired her and had her completely surrounded.

She pulled around to the back of the warehouse, killed the engine, and sat in the car for a long moment.

Colt couldn't blame her. The building was straight out of a nightmare, the kind of place where murderers sought refuge and drug dealers peddled their wares. With the recent spike in human trafficking, Colt was half concerned one of the men skulking around the area would take an interest in Danielle and throw a serious twist into their entire plan, placing her in a triangle between law enforcement, Garcia and an unwitting trafficker.

He clasped and unclasped his fingers. What he wouldn't give to be next to her right now.

When Danielle pushed open the car door, two clicks came over his earpiece—a signal from his team that they were on alert, ready for action. The next sound would be the call to enter the building.

As Danielle crossed the parking lot to the door, Colt prayed. For his teammates, for Justin...

And for Danielle not to be caught in the crossfire.

Danielle's breath shuddered. Every time she tried to inhale, the air fluttered inside her throat, threatening to choke her. Her feet felt heavy in her boots, and trudging across the parking lot was a continual fight for the next step. Tears stung her eyes. How had it come to this?

She was just an average person, a woman trying to raise her brother and make a living. She'd always tried to follow the law, watched too many TV dramas, and drank more coffee than she probably should, just like ninety percent of the other women in America.

But genetics had made her the spitting image of a criminal's sister, and now she was in a battle for her family. Things like this didn't happen to regular people in real life.

Especially not on Christmas Eve. She should be home making hot chocolate and fighting with her brother about whether to watch *It's a Wonderful Life* or *A Christmas Story*. Neither of them should be here, in a battle for their lives instead.

Her insides quaked. Cold sweat slicked her skin as she shuddered against the chill that seeped from her heart into her fingers. She wanted to turn and run to the safety of her car, to drive off into the night and never come back.

But Justin would die if she did. All she wanted was her brother and her home, to go to work and volunteer at the Mission without looking over her shoulder for the rest of her life.

To know for certain that Colt loved her the way she loved him.

All of her dreams hung by a silk thread tonight, with a flame looming ever closer. Within the next hour, her entire future would be decided.

As she reached for the handle at the designated door, Danielle wanted more than anything to turn around and see if she could spot Colt or his team in the bushes or the windows of the building.

But to do that would give them away to anyone

watching. It would signal the end of this mission, the death of her brother, and a possible assault on the men and women who were hidden in the darkness to protect her, placing their lives in harm's way.

Tugging her coat at the hem to insure the small camera in her collar wasn't obscured by a fold, she fought to keep her eyes on the door in front of her. In the next few minutes, she and Justin would either be safe or...

Or she wouldn't think about it. She had to leave this whole thing in God's hands. For years, she'd claimed to have faith. It had never been tested like this.

"Dios mio, ayúdame."

With the quick prayer for help, she pulled the heavy metal door open and stepped inside.

The utter darkness of the room stole her breath.

Something was wrong.

Jenny had pulled up the blueprints for the building and assured Danielle the door she'd entered would lead into the main warehouse, a large cavernous room with windows running along the roofline. This felt small. Too small. The blackness was complete.

Danielle backed toward the door, feeling for the handle so she could get out.

There was none.

Maybe she'd turned herself around and lost track of the door.

She scrambled, running her hands frantically along the corrugated metal wall until she came to the chilled, flat door again. This had to be it, but there was no handle, no lever, no nothing.

She was trapped.

Panic gripped her, driving her legs to move, her body to run. She pounded against the door with her fist, screaming. She was wearing a wire. The Rangers had to hear her. Any second, they'd be here.

A bright light lit the door from behind her, casting her shadow against the green metal.

A deep voice, the accent thick, drifted from behind her. "Adriana. So nice of you to visit."

Danielle pressed her palms against the door and kept her face away from the light. Her heart hammered in her chest so loudly that the man behind her must be able to hear it. She swallowed a revolting mix of fear and bile, trying to force her voice into a normal tone. "I'm here. Let my brother go."

"Let me see your face, *mi hermana*." Footsteps drew closer, the voice sticky with a smooth, false sweetness. "I do not trust these American police. Neither do you, or you would have turned yourself over to them much sooner."

Much sooner. Alarm bells rang in Danielle's head.

He knew she was working with the Rangers. This really was a trap.

Danielle tensed, a gasp escaping before she could stop it. *Please, God. Please let the Rangers hear and get away. Please.*

Behind her, Garcia laughed. "You thought I would not know." An iron grip clutched her elbow and whipped her around, fingers bruising her skin.

The light blinded her, shining close to her face.

A stream of curse words in Spanish blasted through the room, and the hold on her arm tightened, digging in and shooting fire up her arm until she cried out in pain.

"You are not my sister!" the voice roared in Spanish as the man on the other side of the light shook Danielle.

Swinging the hand that held the flashlight, the man

struck the side of her face, whipping her head to the side. Her shoulder struck the wall as stars shot across her vision and the darkness became complete.

NINETEEN

"Move, move, move!" The shout blasted through Colt's earpiece, propelling him toward the building.

Rifle at the ready, he skidded down the embankment to the parking lot and hit the ground running, his boots heavy on the cracked and broken pavement. His heart pounded in his chest. For the call to come so quickly, Danielle must be in trouble.

As the Rangers made themselves known, the handful of drug runners and traffickers in the vicinity fled. Chaos ruled in the parking lot. Everyone on the team tried to make forward progress while eyeing the dozen or so fleeing criminals, trying to make sure Garcia and Danielle weren't among them.

A stream of intel poured through his earpiece. "We've been made. They know we're here. Voice in the room identified as Garcia. Jenny says Danielle's feeds have gone dead."

Ethan Hilliard's last statement almost pitched Colt forward on his face. There were no transmissions from Danielle's wire or camera. Garcia had either found a way to jam them or he had Danielle and had cut them.

From all sides, members of Echo Company and the

special response team flooded the parking lot. A black and white helicopter belonging to the Texas Department of Public Safety swooped in low, its rotors kicking up dust as its searchlights swept the dark areas around the edges of the building. The parking lot was a full combat scene straight out of his worst nightmares overseas.

Danielle and Justin were caught in the middle of it.

It took every ounce of his training to take his assigned role guarding the perimeter and to not kick through the door into that warehouse to rescue Danielle himself. Doing that would only jeopardize the woman he loved—along with every man and woman out here trying to save her. It would result in a slaughter with him as the catalyst.

He had to stick to the plan, even as his feet itched to run directly to where he'd last seen her.

At the corner of the warehouse, Colt took up his position, rifle raised, scanning the dark parking lot and the underbrush beyond. His eyes never stopped moving as his focus stayed fixed on his job. It had to. Too much was at stake.

Movement near the door momentarily stole his attention. Two black-clad members of the SRT unit swung open the door of the SUV Garcia had arrived in and pulled someone out, shielding the person with their body, holding him low as they crossed over to another SUV.

His earpiece hissed. "We have Justin Segovia."

Justin was safe. Exhaling a breath he hadn't realized he'd been holding, Colt watched the area and tried not to track the SUV racing Justin out of danger.

The brush along the edge of the parking lot waved in a slight breeze, but there was no indication anyone hid among the branches. At the top of the hill where he'd taken cover only moments before, a slight rustle was there, then gone. He eyed the spot, saw no further motion, but radioed out anyway. "Movement at southwest corner on the hill."

"On it." Ford Manning's voice crackled back, then Colt's earpiece came to life again.

"There's a room we didn't know about in the building. Target is inside with our asset. No way to enter from inside. Breach from exterior."

Colt's heart hammered faster. For all of the surveillance they'd set up inside the building, Danielle was still alone with Rio Garcia, who'd likely figured out by now that she wasn't Adriana. If those feeds had gone dead because he'd done anything to harm her...

There had to be another way into that room. A man like Rio Garcia would never trap himself inside with only one way out, especially if he knew they were gunning for him on the outside. The man was arrogant, not suicidal.

Colt's leg twitched. This was a setup. A trap. There was another way out and Garcia was likely long gone by now, out of their sight and with Danielle.

Hilliard's voice came across the radio. "Keep your eyes open. This doesn't feel right."

Setting his jaw, Colt tried to keep his focus on the surrounding area, not on the efforts to reach Danielle. *Lord, let her be in there. Let her be safe.*

A loud ping cracked the metal siding only inches to his right.

It was a noise he'd heard one too many times, his mind making the identification and his body diving for cover even as the voice shouted across his radio. "Sniper! Sniper! Southwest corner!"

There was no cover for Colt other than the SUV a few hundred yards away. It was a long haul to safety, but there was no choice. Running toward the guy would be foolish, and Manning was already on his way to take the shooter out. He'd better move quickly, because nobody could breach that door to Danielle's location until the scene was secure.

Watching the area, Colt made a dive for cover. He reached the SUV as a loud crack sounded and pain blasted into his bicep. Dropping, he rolled to safety behind the SUV's tire and pressed his hand to his arm. His glove came back slick with blood.

Brent McCord slid into the small space beside him like he was stealing home, his breath coming heavily. "You okay?"

Colt nodded once, straightening his elbow and flexing his fingers. His arm burned but everything seemed to be working as it should. "Bullet ricocheted off the truck. Just a scratch."

"Seriously? Somebody shot a truck next to you? That's a bad habit, Blackthorn." Brent flashed a quick smile at his own battlefield humor, but another *thwack* cracked against the SUV.

"C'mon, Manning." Colt muttered. Ford had to get to the sniper before he hit someone else. The team was pinned down, and no one could move until the shooter was neutralized.

A sudden silence fell over the large parking lot, louder than any explosion. Colt wanted to peek around the truck but he didn't dare make himself a target. Instead, he assessed his position, his heart beating faster as he realized exactly where he was. In his flight for cover, he'd landed right in front of the door both Garcia and Danielle had used to enter the warehouse.

Elbowing Brent in the arm, Colt tipped his head toward the door. The two of them were the only ones able to reach the door while being blocked from any further shots. With the SUV pulled close to the building to protect Garcia's entrance, it gave them the perfect cover to get inside to Danielle and whoever had her. "You tracking what I'm thinking?"

"Let's do it." Brent nodded with a grim smile. "What's the plan for breaching the door? There's not enough room between the truck and the door to get a good kick in. Not a lock we can shoot, either."

"Cover me. Maybe I can pick it." Colt had acquired a few extra skills over the years. If the lock was old enough, his ID card might make short work of the door.

Moving into position between the end of the building and Colt, Brent trained his weapon into open air, covering them both.

Standing to the side of the door, Colt reached over on a hunch and turned the knob. It twisted easily in his hands. "It's open."

Brent backed into position, his expression hard. This whole thing stunk of a setup. They could open the door and possibly trigger a bomb that would blast the whole building to eternity. There could be two dozen other shooters with their weapons trained at the door.

Anything could happen. They should wait for backup.

Another bullet shattered the rear window of the SUV. Help wasn't coming any time soon, and if they waited any longer, Garcia would escape with Danielle.

"I'm going in."

Brent nodded as Colt threw the door open and stepped into the room, rifle first. The flashlight on the barrel swept the space, landing on three men at the back corner, hauling open a trap door.

"Texas Rangers! Stop where you are!" He kept his light on them although he wanted to swing it around the room. Where was Danielle?

The tallest man whipped around in the small space, squaring off against Colt, who didn't dare fire without knowing where Danielle was.

Adrenaline singing through his veins and throbbing in his wounded arm, Colt kept his weapon trained on the man, praying he wouldn't realize Colt was unwilling to fire his weapon.

A slow, brutal sneer lifted one side of the man's mouth. He knew. Eyes narrowing, he dove at Colt, shoulder down.

Stepping sideways, Colt raised his rifle and brought it down across the man's upper back, slamming him to the ground. Driving his knee into the man's lower back as Brent covered the other men, Colt cuffed him and shoved his cheek against the floor. "Don't try anything."

"Garcia!" Brent's shout cut through the tension as he dove toward the group at the back of the room just as the first man disappeared into the floor. His voice came through the radio. "Pursuing Garcia through a trap door. Blackthorn's staying behind with a suspect."

Brent had lost his mind. He couldn't dive into a hole in the ground in pursuit of unknown suspects without backup. It was stupid and dangerous.

"Sniper down." The radio crackled again. "Move in."

He couldn't wait to back Brent up. Jumping up to

cover Brent's back, Colt swung his rifle around, the flashlight sweeping over a heap on the floor.

Danielle. Colt crossed the small room in two steps and dropped to his knees as light flooded the room and more Rangers entered, most following Brent down the trap door.

Danielle was still. Too still.

Dread flooding his gut, Colt swept the hair from her pale face to find deep red seeping from a gash on her cheek. His arms ached to lift her motionless body from the filthy floor, but someone gripped him from behind and dragged him to his feet away from her as more people entered the room.

His earpiece crackled again. "Asset down."

TWENTY

Colt paced the small private waiting area near the emergency room, constantly watching the door. Medical personnel had separated him from Danielle, but thanks to the bullet graze on his arm, they'd been willing to bring him to the hospital, along with Trevor Street, who'd taken glass to the neck when a bullet shattered one of the windows in the warehouse. The rest of the team remained at the site, sorting out the scene.

He glanced at his phone for the hundredth time. No word from anyone on the status of the mission, on whether or not Brent had successfully brought in Garcia, on the rest of the team...

And no word on either Danielle or Justin's condition. The ambulance transporting Trevor and him had followed hers to the hospital, but he'd been stonewalled ever since because he wasn't family and he had no proof he was officially involved in her case. His arm was nothing more than a nuisance, but Danielle's broken stillness had looked much worse. The way she'd lain there, motionless, haunted him every time he closed his eyes.

"Blackthorn."

Jerking his head up and shoving his phone in his pocket, Colt found Brent McCord standing in the doorway. Cobwebs and dirt streaked his black tactical uniform, and dark smudges of dust covered his face. His eyes wore a haunted look Colt recognized well.

Failure. Defeat. The twins to the ache in his own soul.

"You okay?" Colt crossed the room to the man who used to be his friend, the one who'd had his back without question in the fight tonight, the way it should be.

"Garcia got away. I don't know how. The tunnel was dark, took a few turns…" Brent shrugged and sank into a chair, staring at the floor. "We took the guy you grabbed into custody and managed to apprehend one other. Both say Garcia knows Danielle isn't Adriana, which is good news, but I missed him. I had him and I let him go."

"Not just you." Colt dropped into the chair beside Brent but kept one eye on the door. "We all did. We missed the extra room in the building, the escape tunnel… Garcia's good, but he's going to slip up eventually and we're going to catch him."

"But will we catch him before he finds the real Adriana?" Brent lifted his head and pinned Colt with an almost desperate gaze. "I know you think she's the one who killed Greg, but my gut says the evidence is too convenient." He held up a hand to ward off any argument Colt might lob at him. "I know you don't think you can know someone after only—"

"I've been thinking about that."

Brent stopped, eyeing him warily. "Meaning, what, exactly?"

"Meaning I see how fast someone can work their way into your head. I spent a lot of time wrapped up in myself, and—"

"And trying to save every kid on the street, which you can't do."

"I know that now. Those kids Justin's been running with… There's a thousand more like them. And even if I saved every single one of them, it wouldn't bring Caleb back."

"Who's Caleb?"

He'd forgotten how little he spoke of his brother. "That's a longer story than we have time for now. What I was saying was, I guess I can see now how Adriana Garcia has you convinced she's innocent." He held up one finger in a "wait a minute" gesture. "I'm not prepared to say she's never done anything wrong, but I'm willing to wait until we have real proof of guilt."

Brent seemed to read Colt's expression for a moment before he stood and paced across the room, hands shoved in his pockets. He stared out the window for a long time before he spoke again. "I'm going after her. Those notes that Vance keeps dismissing? I believe there's something to them. They're coming straight to me. Only someone who knew we'd run into each other before would target me. It's not a coincidence."

This had been coming for a long time. The entire time they'd been locking horns over this, it had been obvious Brent wouldn't be able to leave it alone. Colt could keep fighting his friend, or he could accept it and be a part of the solution. "I understand."

"You're the one I expected to try and stop me."

"Sometimes you do things you never thought you would."

Brent sniffed and chuckled. "You're in love with Danielle Segovia."

There it was. Concrete words out in the air. He could confirm it or deny it, but the truth was the truth. "I am."

"I knew it." The voice at the door whipped both men around.

Justin stood there, a half smile cocked on his face. "I was just waiting for one of you to say it."

Half of the tension in Colt's shoulders melted. "Justin." With a glance at Brent, Colt crossed the room and studied the young man closer. Despite the smile on his face, Justin's eyes were haunted, his skin pale in the fluorescent lights. "You okay?"

Justin seemed to consider his words before he spoke. "They didn't hurt me. The Garcia guy, for some crazy reason he thought I was his brother. Said his father was never faithful. He wouldn't let anyone touch me. But having a gun pointed at your head…" He visibly shuddered and looked unseeing at something over Colt's shoulder.

It would take some time, some counseling even, to get over the psychological trauma he'd likely endured over the course of the past few hours.

Colt intended to be there to help.

"So, about my sister…" Justin scratched his cheek, then stared down at the floor. "I'm sorry I told you to back off. I guess I wanted to be the big man of the house when really, I was wrong. All wrong. You were right to get in my face the way you did."

"I'd do it again, too." Colt answered the unspoken

request to be involved in the young man's life. As much as he loved Danielle, he knew he cared about her brother like he'd cared about his own. "I'm not going anywhere, not if you guys will have me."

"I'm good with that. Danielle might take some convincing, though." Justin looked up suddenly and grinned. "Just kidding. She's in room 318, asking for you."

Brent outright laughed, then slapped Colt on the back, jarring his still burning arm where stitches pulled tight against his skin. "You'd better get to stepping, Blackthorn, before some hot male nurse catches her eye."

"I'll be praying you find Adriana." The words were awkward in Colt's mouth, but they were sincere.

Brent nodded. "We're good. I'll contact you if I need anything."

"Be safe." It was the best Colt could do, torn between his friend and the woman he loved.

"Always. Now get out of here."

Colt didn't have to be told twice. It took all of his self-control not to run down the hallway. He kept it to a slow jog, stopping at the door to Danielle's room and steadying his breath before he went in. No need to scare her.

Just as she had only a few days earlier—had it really only been a few days?—she reclined in the bed with her eyes closed. A bandage covered her cheek where the gash had been. Her dark hair fanned across the white pillow. Her face was pale but Colt knew now what he'd been unwilling to admit for too long. Danielle Segovia was the most beautiful woman he'd ever seen.

* * *

"We really should stop meeting like this."

The deep voice at the door, husky with emotion, washed over Danielle. Her eyes flew open. "Colt."

The heart monitor beside her registered her spiking heart rate. He was safe. He was here. He'd come for her. "You're okay. The paramedics said you were shot."

"Ricochet scratched my arm. No big deal. Only half a dozen stitches." He took two hesitant steps into the room. "You were the one who had me scared." Sinking to the edge of the bed, he lifted one of her hands, his fingers warm and strong around hers.

"They're keeping me overnight, but I'll be okay, especially now that I know…" She swallowed the words, afraid of saying too much. If the past few days had been nothing more than an emotional reaction for either of them, she didn't want to look like a fool now.

Colt ran his thumb along her wrist, back and forth, the light touch running up her arm and fluttering in her stomach. His eyes never left hers, and his voice dropped low. "Garcia knows you're not his sister. You're safe now. So's Justin."

Relief flooded her, but it blended with the warmth of his touch in a flurry of mixed emotions. Would that kiss, those warm moments, all disappear now that her life could go back to normal? Now that she was no longer Colt's job, would he disappear?

Their time together had been short, but if he walked out of her life now, she would never be the same again. But how to put that into words escaped her, especially with the way that slow stroke of his thumb on her wrist was dancing across her heart and clouding her thinking, stealing her will to keep silent.

"Colt?"

He was still searching her face, his dark eyes filled with something she hoped against hope she was reading correctly. "Yes?"

It was now or never. If she let him walk out tonight and didn't tell him what she felt, she would regret it for the rest of her life. "That first night you came in my shop, when you said your name was Beckett?"

His eyebrow arched in question, but he said nothing, just eased closer to her.

This wasn't fair. He had an advantage because he could see her heart rate on the monitor beside the bed. He was bound to know it was pounding so hard the nurses ought to be rushing in.

She swallowed. "I did something I never do."

"What's that?" With his free hand, he brushed her hair gently from her forehead and let his fingers trail down her face. If he didn't stop, she'd lose the ability to speak.

"Checked to see if you were wearing a ring."

He threw his head back and laughed. For the first time since she'd met him, the sound of his true, real, full laugh washed over her. She'd give anything to hear it again and again. It seemed to drop a weight from him. The lines around his eyes were eased in joy instead of sorrow.

His eyes...so dark, pinned directly on her as his laughter faded and his expression shifted to something much, much warmer. "Even though I was certain you weren't who you said you were, you were still the most beautiful woman I'd ever seen."

"You still think that?"

"Definitely." Sliding closer, he took both of her hands

in his and leaned forward, locking her fingers behind his neck and pressing his forehead gently against hers. "And I love you, Danielle Segovia." His voice was a low murmur on lips that brushed hers gently, then came back to capture them in a kiss that raced from his lips straight to her heart.

EPILOGUE

Christmas Day

The day could not end fast enough.

Outside her apartment, Danielle rested her head on the cool door and held her keys limp at her side, almost too tired to turn them in the lock. She hadn't stopped since yesterday, and her body demanded rest.

Once the doctors had released her from the hospital, Colt had driven her to headquarters to answer questions until her brain scrambled. At some point while she was telling her story for the second time, he'd been called away, leaving Kylie to bring her home.

Pulling in a deep breath, Danielle turned and waved to the other woman that it was okay to go as she tried to readjust her thinking. She'd refused Kylie's offer to walk her to the door, knowing the danger was over and it was time to stand on her own two feet again, even if her brain still screamed she was in danger.

No one would be staying at her home tonight. No one would be watching from the parking lot. She was a regular citizen again.

A regular citizen who was in love with a Ranger.

Hopefully, he'd call soon, the way he'd promised when he left her earlier. She already missed having him around, and the prospect of alone time wasn't exactly thrilling at the moment.

Even Justin wouldn't be home for a couple of hours. The Rangers weren't done debriefing him yet. She'd been reluctant to leave him after all that had happened, but Kylie had all but ordered her to come home.

This had to be the most twisted Christmas she'd ever known. With a wry smile, Danielle shoved the key into the lock and turned it. So be it. They could have turkey and presents tomorrow. Thanks to Colt and the rest of the Rangers, there was a tomorrow to look forward to.

A soft glow from the corner of the room stopped her with one foot inside the door and one foot out. While she was no longer a target for the Garcia cartel, her heart still held the closet terror that life could spin out of control at any moment, and it ramped into overdrive.

The enormous Christmas tree in the corner twinkled with lights Danielle knew she hadn't left lit.

The spicy scent of pumpkin pie drifted and... Was that turkey?

When her pulse pounded harder, it had nothing to do with fear.

Colt. What was he up to now?

Sure enough, when she shoved the door open all the way, he stood in the kitchen holding two plates, his eyes wide with surprise. "You weren't supposed to be here for another half hour." The bright red shirt he wore made him look even more amazing than usual.

She smiled, the sight of him jolting through her with an anticipation she couldn't identify. "I can leave."

"Don't you dare." Sliding the plates onto the counter,

he wiped his hands down his jeans and gave her one of those looks that always made her knees week. "Justin got the apartment manager to let me in. I wanted to surprise you, but…"

"Oh, I'm surprised." The words came out in a whisper, the fatigue that had dragged her down earlier lifting with his presence. "So, this is what called you away?"

When he reached her side, he slipped her purse from her arm and tossed it on the couch, then wrapped both arms around her waist and pulled her close, pressing a kiss to her hair before pulling away slightly. "I was doing some thinking. Garcia stole so much from you and Justin, that there was no way I was letting him steal your Christmas, too, not when I know how much it means to you. The guys will drop Justin off in about an hour to eat with us, if that's okay." He tipped his head toward the tree, though his eyes never left hers. "Merry Christmas."

Emotion threatened to choke her. In the hospital, he'd told her repeatedly how much he loved her. This took every one of his words and wrapped them in a bow. Swallowing tears, she pressed a hand to his cheek. "I didn't have time to buy you a present."

A smile, wide, boyish and loaded with secrets, lifted his lips. "I can tell you what I want."

The tone of his voice sent the best kind of shivers up her spine as he took her hand and led her to the tree. He stood behind her, one arm around her waist and his chest against her back, then leaned forward to aim his finger at a small, sparkling ornament that dangled from a slim red ribbon.

"You can say yes."

Danielle's next breath caught in her throat. That was

no ornament. Lifting her hand, she cradled the platinum ring in her hand. A deep red emerald-cut stone flanked by two diamonds winked at her, then blurred behind a haze of tears.

Lifting the ring from her hand, Colt untied the ribbon and wrapped his arms around her, pulling her back against his chest as he held the ring up for her to see. "A Mexican fire opal. You needed something different than a diamond." His voice whispered against her hair. "Something more you. It's been through literal fire and come out even more beautiful."

His heart pounded against her back as wildly as hers did. It had been such a short time since he'd first walked into her shop believing she was a criminal, but she knew without a doubt... He was the man God had created for her. "I love you."

He chuckled softly, the warmth of his breath on her cheek sending chills along her skin. "I love you, too." Turning her toward him, he pulled her closer and looked down, his eyes capturing hers. "So do I get a yes for Christmas?"

Danielle nodded once, but before she could speak, his lips were on hers, full of promise and full of forever.

* * * * *

*If you enjoyed CHRISTMAS DOUBLE CROSS,
be sure to get the next book in the*
TEXAS RANGER HOLIDAY *series—*
*TEXAS CHRISTMAS DEFENDER
by Elizabeth Goddard*

*And don't miss a book in the series:
THANKSGIVING PROTECTOR
by Sharon Dunn
CHRISTMAS DOUBLE CROSS
by Jodie Bailey
TEXAS CHRISTMAS DEFENDER
by Elizabeth Goddard*

Find more great reads at www.LoveInspired.com.

Dear Reader,

As I type this, I'm sitting on my couch watching it rain. Yesterday was the first day of 2017—though by the time you hold this in your hands, we'll already be looking forward to 2018. I spend a lot of time thinking about the word "new" in my life, and how Jesus said He "makes all things new."

To me, that is the most beautiful thing Christ ever said. I mean, really…our old is pretty rotten. The fact that Jesus takes our rotten old and makes it a fresh, new, beautiful thing constantly amazes me. It's the theme of my life, repeated over and over.

It seems to show up in every book I write, even this one. Colt was in need of a big ol' batch of "new." He couldn't let go of the misplaced guilt of his past. He couldn't grasp the love of Jesus because he was so buried in his own hurt. Then God sent him someone to show him love…not only the love of another person but to usher him right back to the true love of Christ.

New.

Are you in need of a big dose of "new"? Believe me, nobody's so far gone that Jesus can't provide that cleansing, beautiful newness. As you look around at a more mature 2017 than I'm looking at, take a minute, set this book aside, and ask God what kind of new He has planned for you.

It will definitely be incredible. I'd love to hear all about it! Drop me a line at jodie@jodiebailey.com or swing by the website at www.jodiebailey.com and say hello. You're awesome. Thanks for hanging out!

COMING NEXT MONTH FROM
Love Inspired® Suspense

Available December 5, 2017

CLASSIFIED K-9 UNIT CHRISTMAS
Classified K-9 Unit • by Lenora Worth and Terri Reed
When danger strikes at Christmastime, two K-9 FBI agents meet their perfect matches in these exciting, brand-new novellas.

CHRISTMAS RANCH RESCUE
Wrangler's Corner • by Lynette Eason and Lauryn Eason
When his former crush, Becca Price, is suspected of funneling drugs through her ranch, DEA agent Nathan Williams is sent to spy on her. But after she's attacked, he knows she's innocent. Now he just has to prove it—and keep her alive.

TEXAS CHRISTMAS DEFENDER
Texas Ranger Holidays • by Elizabeth Goddard
Texas Ranger Brent McCord is convinced the woman who saved his life while he was undercover in Mexico can't be a murderer. But since Adriana Garcia *did* steal drugs and money from her drug-kingpin brother, clearing her name and protecting her may be more difficult than he expects.

HOLIDAY SECRETS
McKade Law • by Susan Sleeman
Back in his hometown for an investigation, FBI agent Gavin McKade discovers the man he's come to question—his ex-girlfriend's father—has been murdered. And with the killer after Lexie Grant, his new mission is to safeguard the woman whose heart he broke when he left town.

AMISH CHRISTMAS ABDUCTION
Amish Country Justice • by Dana R. Lynn
After an Amish toddler who'd been kidnapped by a smuggling ring stows away in her car, widowed single mom Irene Martello and her little boys are in danger...and their only hope of survival is turning to her former sweetheart, local police chief Paul Kennedy, for help.

YULETIDE SUSPECT
Secret Service Agents • by Lisa Phillips
Someone has kidnapped a senator and two White House staff members, and former Secret Service agent Tate Almers is the top suspect. His ex-fiancée, Secret Service agent Liberty Westmark, is sure he's being framed, though, and she'll risk everything to help him bring down the real culprits.

LOOK FOR THESE AND OTHER LOVE INSPIRED BOOKS WHEREVER BOOKS ARE SOLD, INCLUDING MOST BOOKSTORES, SUPERMARKETS, DISCOUNT STORES AND DRUGSTORES.

LISCNM1117

Get 2 Free Books,
Plus 2 Free Gifts—
just for trying the Reader Service!

 *Love Inspired* SUSPENSE

YES! Please send me 2 FREE Love Inspired® Suspense novels and my 2 FREE mystery gifts (gifts are worth about $10 retail). After receiving them, if I don't wish to receive any more books, I can return the shipping statement marked "cancel." If I don't cancel, I will receive 4 brand-new novels every month and be billed just $5.24 each for the regular-print edition or $5.74 each for the larger-print edition in the U.S., or $5.74 each for the regular-print edition or $6.24 each for the larger-print edition in Canada. That's a savings of at least 13% off the cover price. It's quite a bargain! Shipping and handling is just 50¢ per book in the U.S. and 75¢ per book in Canada.* I understand that accepting the 2 free books and gifts places me under no obligation to buy anything. I can always return a shipment and cancel at any time. The free books and gifts are mine to keep no matter what I decide.

Please check one: ☐ Love Inspired Suspense Regular-Print   ☐ Love Inspired Suspense Larger-Print
                   (153/353 IDN GLW2)   (107/307 IDN GLW2)

Name	(PLEASE PRINT)	
Address		Apt. #
City	State/Prov.	Zip/Postal Code
Signature (if under 18, a parent or guardian must sign)		

Mail to the **Reader Service:**
IN U.S.A.: P.O. Box 1341, Buffalo, NY 14240-8531
IN CANADA: P.O. Box 603, Fort Erie, Ontario L2A 5X3

**Want to try two free books from another line?
Call 1-800-873-8635 or visit www.ReaderService.com.**

* Terms and prices subject to change without notice. Prices do not include applicable taxes. Sales tax applicable in N.Y. Canadian residents will be charged applicable taxes. Offer not valid in Quebec. This offer is limited to one order per household. Books received may not be as shown. Not valid for current subscribers to Love Inspired Suspense books. All orders subject to approval. Credit or debit balances in a customer's account(s) may be offset by any other outstanding balance owed by or to the customer. Please allow 4 to 6 weeks for delivery. Offer available while quantities last.

Your Privacy—The Reader Service is committed to protecting your privacy. Our Privacy Policy is available online at www.ReaderService.com or upon request from the Reader Service.

We make a portion of our mailing list available to reputable third parties that offer products we believe may interest you. If you prefer that we not exchange your name with third parties, or if you wish to clarify or modify your communication preferences, please visit us at www.ReaderService.com/consumerchoice or write to us at Reader Service Preference Service, P.O. Box 9062, Buffalo, NY 14240-9062. Include your complete name and address.

LIS17R2